PEN PALS:
BOOK SEVENTEEN

THE BOY PROJECT

by Sharon Dennis Wyeth

A YEARLING BOOK

Published by
Dell Publishing
a division of
Bantam Doubleday Dell Publishing Group, Inc.
666 Fifth Avenue
New York, New York 10103

Illustrations by Wendy Wax
The trademark Yearling ® is registered in the U.S. Patent and Trademark Office.
The trademark Dell® is registered in the U.S. Patent and Trademark Office.
ISBN: 0-440-40493-2

Published by arrangement with Parachute Press, Inc.
Printed in the United States of America
July 1991
10 9 8 7 6 5 4 3 2 1
OPM

For Aunt Carolyn and Uncle Emmett

PEN PALS:
BOOK SEVENTEEN

THE BOY PROJECT

CHAPTER ONE

"Guess what? I have the most amazing news!" Nimbly balancing her books and lunch tray, Shanon Davis dashed across the dining hall at the Alma Stephens School for Girls just outside Brighton, N.H.

"You won't believe it," she said breathlessly to her three suitemates. "A boy is coming to live at Alma for three whole weeks!"

"A boy? At Alma?" Palmer Durand pushed back her long, wavy blond hair. "*Major* improvement . . . but why only one?"

"Hot news!" Maxie Schloss chimed in. "Who is he? Where is he from?"

"He must be from another planet, if he really wants to live at Alma," Amy Ho said with a giggle.

"He's from the Pewter School," Shanon explained, mentioning an all-boys boarding school just across the Massachusetts state line. She slipped off her heavy backpack and took a seat. "He's the editor of *The Pewter Bugle*, and he's coming to do a story comparing his school with ours. The teachers, classes, social life—"

"Social life?" Palmer cut in. "There's more social life at my grandma's senior citizen community."

"Don't worry, Palmer. A guy on campus will definitely liven things up around here!" Maxie said. "When is he coming?"

"Mr. Griffith didn't know for sure," Shanon replied. "But that's not all my news," she continued in a rush. "Remember that project I had to do for Mr. Griffith's video-journalism class?"

"He wanted you to enter a video in some sort of contest?" Amy recalled.

"Right. There's a state-wide competition for high school students. Mr. Griffith thought I should enter, but I couldn't come up with a good idea."

"So? What does that have to do with the guy from Pewter?" Palmer said, obviously more eager to talk about boys than schoolwork.

"The guy from Pewter is going to be my project," Shanon announced brightly. "I'm going to videotape his entire visit to Alma."

"What a great idea!" Amy said.

"That's really neat," Maxie agreed. "It will be like a documentary. A stranger in a strange land," she added, slipping into a spacey voice. "Alma Stephens . . . the final frontier. . . . This is the story of one brave guy from Pewter who dared journey where no boy has ever been before!"

"Remind me to call you in when I'm ready for the voice-overs," Shanon said, tousling her roommate's already tousled red curls.

"I think it will make a really cool video," Amy enthused.

"*If* our visitor from Pewter is cool," Palmer said. "I hope he's not a freshman. Older boys are so much more interesting."

"Maybe he'll be in some of our classes," Maxie said.

"Maybe he'll live in our dorm!" Amy said. "That would be truly wild."

"Maybe he'll look like Tom Cruise," Palmer said wistfully. "I hope he's at least cute. It would be such a waste if he wasn't."

"I just hope he agrees to my idea," Shanon said. "He might not want to do it."

"Don't worry, he'll do it," Amy said encouragingly. "It's flattering to think that somebody wants to follow you around night and day with a camera—"

"Like Prince Charles or something," Palmer cut in. "Personally, I think Andrew is definitely the cuter prince. Charles has such weird ears."

"What in the world do Prince Charles's ears have to do with this guy from Pewter?" Amy said, turning to look at Palmer.

"What did you say his name was?" Maxie asked Shanon.

"It's Fenimore . . . Fenimore Hudson," Shanon replied, her voice trailing off to nearly a whisper.

"Fenimore!?" Maxie clasped her hand over her mouth to smother her giggles.

"You're joking, right?" Amy asked, giggling now, too.

"I knew this sounded too good to be true," Palmer said. "With a name like Fenimore he probably *does* have weird ears!"

"Well, with a name like that I doubt that he'll look much like Tom Cruise," Maxie said. "Sounds like a definite nerd alert to me. Especially if he's the editor of the school paper."

"What's wrong with working on the school newspaper?" Shanon said indignantly. "*I* work on the Alma paper, you know."

"No offense, Shanon." Amy patted her friend on the shoulder. "You're a terrific reporter. I love reading your articles in *The Ledger*. But this guy from Pewter is starting to sound like he might be a bit on the dweeby side."

"You're not being very fair," Shanon said, punctuating her remark with a big bite of a crisp red apple. "You haven't even met the guy."

"With a name like Sycamore—I mean Fenimore—I'm not sure I want to," Maxie quipped, giggling again.

"Good point," Palmer said, rolling her big blue eyes.

"Well, I'm still going to write to him," Shanon told the others.

"Speaking of letters," Palmer said. "I almost forgot. I stopped off at Booth Hall for the mail on my way over." She dug through her purse and came up with two letters. "One for Max from Paul and one for Shanon from Mars."

Palmer handed each girl a letter and they eagerly tore them open. When the suitemates had first come to Alma the year before, they had advertised for pen pals in the newspaper run by the students at Ardsley Academy, a nearby boys' prep school. Code-naming themselves the Foxes of the Third Dimension because they all lived in Suite 3-D of Fox Hall, the girls had received many responses. The most interesting were from four boys who called themselves The Unknown and who became their first pen pals. Some of the girls had switched pen pals several times since

4

then, but they all still shared their letters with each other—and they still thought of their group as the Foxes.

"Did you get anything, Palmer?" Amy asked.

"Just a postcard from my father. He's on a business trip in Geneva," she reported with a frown. "I don't get it."

"You don't understand why your father's in Geneva? He probably has a client there," Amy suggested logically.

"Not that. I don't understand why everybody got a letter from their pen pal this week but me. I guess I made a fool of myself writing to Rain again."

Rain Blackburn was Maxie's cousin, whom Palmer had met at Maxie's during winter vacation. She had immediately developed a crush on the older, sophisticated boy, and wrote him many long letters over the past few months. Everyone but Palmer had noticed that his few notes in reply were polite but hardly encouraging. A few weeks ago, however, he had sent her a postcard with a Renoir painting on the front. The woman in the painting had long wavy blond hair, and Rain wrote that she reminded him of Palmer. That small comment had kept Palmer on cloud nine for weeks, but now it seemed her cloud was slowly but surely floating back to earth.

"Why did you do that?" Amy said. "I thought he didn't even answer your last letter."

"That's because it probably got lost in the mail or something," Palmer said, smoothing down her teal-blue suede skirt. "New York is a big place, Amy."

"I know exactly how big New York is. I live there, remember?" Born in Taiwan, Amy had lived in many places around the world before her family finally settled in New York City.

"Maybe it did get lost," Shanon chimed in sympathetically. "You never know. Or maybe he wrote you and *his* letter got lost."

"Maybe," Palmer said gratefully. Tall and beautiful and very rich, Palmer was used to getting whatever—or *whomever*—she wanted. Rain was the first boy who had ever presented her with much of a challenge.

"I would be the ideal girlfriend for Rain." Palmer sighed. "If only I could make him see that we're a perfect match."

"I bet you'll get something from him tomorrow," Shanon said sympathetically. "But in the meantime, let's read our letters," she said, holding up a square white envelope.

"And I have a letter from Paul," Maxie said happily.

"Well, let's hear them both," Palmer replied. "Shanon first."

Dear Shanon,

Did I tell you I am taking Japanese this term as a language elective? I am sitting in my class right this very minute, thinking about pizza. Don't ask me why, but I always get a craving for pizza when I speak Japanese. Someday I would like to take a long trip around the world and sample the junk-food delicacies of each country. Traveling mainly by skateboard, of course. It would be definitely slow but possibly newsworthy. If you've become a famous reporter by then, perhaps you'd like to interview me?—Mars Martinez, first man to circum-skateboard the globe!

Seriously, I hope all is well at good old Alma. I liked the piece you wrote for The Ledger *last week about literacy volunteers. It's an important cause and maybe your article will inspire more kids to volunteer. Good work, Lois Lane!*

Uh-oh, my teacher-san is giving me a dirty look. Time to beam down to class. (When are we going to learn how to say really useful stuff, like extra cheese, no pepperoni?) Write soon.

Sayonara
Mars-san

"Cute," Palmer said, not sounding very impressed. "Mars can be pretty funny sometimes."

"He does have a good sense of humor," Amy agreed.

It was a typical letter from Mars, Shanon thought. Funny, sweet, and even complimentary. But for some reason this and his last few letters had left her feeling let down instead of perked up. She really like Mars. . . . Sometimes she even thought she loved him. And on the rare occasions that she got to see him, he seemed to feel the same way about her. But you'd never know it from his letters, she thought now. Especially the last few. Shanon would eagerly race through his breezy little notes, looking for some hint of romance amidst the zany jokes and friendly chatter. She rarely seemed to find any. Shanon was starting to wonder if Mars had any romantic interest at all in her, or if he considered her only a very good friend. Maybe he—

Shanon broke off her musing as she suddenly became conscious that three pairs of curious eyes were fixed on her. She knew her friends could tell something was up, but she really didn't want to talk about it.

"Did you and Mars have a fight?" Amy asked gently.

"No, nothing like that." Shanon tossed back her sandy-colored hair and forced a small smile. "I'm just in a strange mood today, I guess. His jokes don't seem as funny to me as usual."

7

"Even the best comics have a bad day," Maxie offered, and Shanon flashed her a genuine smile. Maxie's father, Max Schloss, was a famous comedian who had his own TV show. Some days he was hysterical. Some days just funny. And every once in a while he told the same corny jokes as any other father.

"I guess you're right," Shanon said, folding the letter and slipping it into her notebook. "What about your letter from Paul?" she asked, happy to change the subject.

"No offense," Palmer piped up. "But I hope Maxie's letter is juicier than yours."

"It's mostly about brains. So I guess that's pretty juicy," Maxie joked, blushing a little. Having a boy pen pal was still a new experience for her. It was exciting but scary, too. With her curly red hair, green eyes, and slim build, Maxie often attracted attention from boys. But she was secretly quite shy and hid that fact behind her jokes and clowning.

"Here—you read it, Palmer," Maxie said. "I feel silly reading this out loud."

"No problem." Sitting up straight, Palmer theatrically cleared her throat and began:

Dear Maxie,
   Thanks for your letter last week. It really cheered me up. I would have written back sooner, but I've been working every spare minute on my term project for advanced bio. It's an experiment on the electric charges generated by the human brain. It's complicated to explain, but if it comes out well, Ms. Samuelson, my bio teacher, wants me to enter it in the national science fair. (Hope all this is not too boring, but you did mention that you liked science, too.)

Good news—I made the cut for the baseball team! The coach has me pitching, which is really cool, and the guys on the team say I have a mean curveball. Wish you could see me play sometime. Maybe we could work on it?

Got to go! (I hear Mars banging on the door—must've lost his keys again. He is the original space cadet.) Brainlessly awaiting your next letter—

Paul

P.S. Did you know that the brain's electrical activity varies depending on what you think about?

P.P.S. You are definitely in the "high voltage" category for me.

"Wow!" Shanon said, raising an eyebrow at Paul's closing line. Why didn't Mars ever write things like that to her? "I'd better put a sign on our door. DANGER—HIGH VOLTAGE," she teased Maxie.

"Shanon! He was just making a joke," Maxie said, turning an even brighter shade of red.

"High voltage, huh?" Amy said, giggling. "Some joke!"

"Paul really likes you, Maxie," Palmer pronounced. "It's official."

"Come on," Maxie protested. "He hardly knows me."

"That never stopped anybody from liking a person," Amy said, thinking about her own mega-crush on Nikos Smith, another Ardie.

Amy and Nikos had exchanged only one letter so far. He had written to her a few weeks ago, explaining that he'd been watching her play softball all season and really wanted to get to know her. And Amy, who had noticed him at the last Alma-Ardsley mixer, had gladly written back.

9

"I'd better get going," she said now, glancing at her watch. "I have to drop off some books at the library on my way to class."

"Wait up. I'll walk you over," Maxie said, quickly scooping up her books. "Want to come with us, Shanon?"

"Uh, no thanks," Shanon said. "I think I'll just hang out here for a while. See you later."

"Wait for me," Palmer said, checking her appearance in a small mirror she slipped out of her purse. "I think I'll run up to the suite before class. I feel like changing my blouse. This one makes me look fat."

"Fat? Palmer, you're crazy." Amy giggled, giving her willowy roommate an affectionate glance.

"Go ahead and laugh," Palmer replied coolly, "but I don't think anyone would expect me to take fashion advice from a person whose favorite item of clothing is a black T-shirt that says, 'This is a Nuclear Free Zone.' "

"Never mind." Amy shook her head. "You look great the way you are. Let's just get going." And turning to Shanon, she said, "See you later."

As soon as her friends left the dining hall, Shanon fished Mars's letter out of her notebook and read it again. Then she opened her history notebook to a clean page and began to write:

Dear Mars . . .

Shanon put her pen down with a sigh. She couldn't help thinking about Maxie's letter from Paul. Maxie hardly knew Paul and he was already writing really sweet things to her. Why couldn't Mars ever show his feelings like that?

She crumpled up the paper and tossed it into her empty

soup bowl. She didn't feel like writing Mars tonight. Maybe she'd do it tomorrow.

Turning to a new page, Shanon chewed on the tip of her pen and tried to think of just the right way to begin another letter—a much more interesting letter than one to her dear, sweet, predictable old friend Mars.

CHAPTER TWO

Dear Fenimore Hudson,

 I am a student at Alma Stephens. One of my teachers, Mr. Dan Griffith, told me that you will soon be coming here to research an article for The Pewter Bugle. I think your idea—comparing a boys' school like Pewter with a girls' school like Alma—is truly terrific. I will be very interested to learn what you discover. As a reporter for my own school newspaper, The Ledger, I am writing to ask you a very important favor. I would like to videotape your stay at Alma as a special project for my video-journalism class. As a fellow journalist, I hope you can see how this would be a great story for me. Hoping to hear from you soon.

Best wishes,
Shanon Davis

Shanon read her letter over and added another line:

P.S. Even if you decide not to do it, I still look forward to meeting you when you come to Alma Stephens.

12

She sealed the letter, wondering if she was setting herself up for a disaster. If Fenimore was a total nerd, she'd feel like a total fool, following him around with a video camera. Oh, well, she thought philosophically. The movie *Revenge of the Nerds* had been a big hit. Maybe she'd be the first fourteen-year-old girl to do a video documentary on a dweeby guy at an all-girls boarding school.

Shanon did not have too long to wait for Fenimore Hudson's reply. Three days later, on Friday afternoon, she was sitting in The Tuck Shop with Amy and Maxie, splitting a Super-Oink sundae, when Palmer raced up to their table with a fistful of letters.

"Time out from your pig-out, ladies," Palmer commanded cheerfully. "Mail call!"

Shanon, Amy, and Maxie shared a secret look. They more than suspected that Palmer's high spirits meant she'd just gotten a letter from Rain Blackburn.

"A Pewter School return address," Palmer chirped as she handed out the letters—one for Amy from her brother, one for Maxie from her parents, and the last one for Shanon. "*Who* could be writing to you from Pewter?" she asked archly.

"I guess it's from Fenimore Hudson," Shanon said casually. "I'll read it later."

"Say-no-more, it's Fen-i-more," Maxie quipped, doing a drumroll with her ice-cream spoon.

"Hey, I think there's a tune in there somewhere," Amy announced, tapping out a rap beat with her own spoon. "Say-no-more, it's Fen-i-more. He's-a-bore. I-think-we're-sure, old-Fen-i-more will-make-us-snore."

The girls exploded into laughter. All except Shanon. "I

13

think I'll head back to the dorm now," she said. "See you later."

Her suitemates were instantly sorry they'd teased her.

"Hey, Shanon. Don't leave. We were only joking," Maxie apologized. "You've hardly touched your share of the Oink."

"Sorry, Shanon. Guess I got carried away," Amy said, still giggling a little. "Even if he is a bore, I'm sure your video on him won't be."

"Come on, Shanon. Read it out loud. We want to hear if Sycamore—I mean Fenimore—said yes," Palmer prodded.

"Okay, I give up." Shanon pulled out the letter. It was short and to the point. She scanned it quickly, then passed it to the others so they could read it for themselves.

Dear Shanon,

Your letter was a pleasant surprise. I thought my visit to Alma was top secret. I am glad to hear a fellow journalist likes my idea. Your video project sounds interesting, too. I'd be honored to be your subject. I am arriving at Alma on Monday. Let's talk more about it then.

Yours truly,
Fen Hudson

"He sounds older than I thought," Amy said. "I bet he's at least a fourth-former."

"Older and . . . well, a lot less dweeby," Maxie agreed, spooning up a glob of ice cream and hot fudge.

"He doesn't sound at *all* dweeby to me," Shanon said happily. "He sounds very mature."

14

"He sounds all right, I guess," Palmer said, flipping the letter back in Shanon's direction. "Of course, he's not anywhere near as mature as Rain," she added. "Rain is *so* mature, *so* sophisticated, *so*—"

"So slow at writing back?" Amy cut in.

"He happened to have missed my letters," Palmer said nonchalantly. "And he apologized very sweetly for the delay."

"You got a letter from Rain? What did he say?" Shanon asked.

"He's been away," Palmer said. "He took two weeks extra after spring break to visit his father in California. He worked on a real movie set and got school credit. Did you know his father is a famous movie director?"

"Maybe Rain's father will put you in the movies, Palmer," Amy teased her. "A horror movie about a girl who can't stop shopping."

Seeing the look on Palmer's face, Maxie, Amy, and Shanon started giggling so hard they almost choked on their ice cream.

"Our room already looks like the set of a horror movie—one that takes place in a haunted gymnasium with all your sports equipment all over the place," Palmer replied huffily. "I couldn't even find my hot rollers this morning. I had to wear my hair in a ponytail today."

"What a crisis! An unscheduled hairdo!" Amy shrieked in mock horror.

"The hairstyle did not go with my outfit at all." Palmer gave her friends an exasperated frown. Then, looking at the clock over the snack bar, she jumped up from the table. "I'd better get going. I've got some work to do in the library."

"Studying? On a Friday night?" Maxie said in a stunned voice.

"Palmer, do you feel okay?" Amy asked her.

"Gosh, can't a person try to catch up on their homework without getting interrogated? I'm working on a special . . . research project," she said innocently. "Uh, before I forget," she added, pausing at Maxie's chair, "remember you once told me that Rain is crazy about cars?"

Maxie nodded. "Especially expensive, foreign ones."

"Any kind in particular?" Palmer asked.

Maxie thought for a moment. "I think he told me once that the Lamborghini was his favorite. Why do you ask?"

"Oh, no real reason. I was just wondering. And what about those songs he played at your party? He told me the name of a composer he liked, but I can't remember it now."

"Gershwin?"

"That's it!" Palmer said. "See you guys later," she said cheerfully.

As soon as Palmer was out of earshot, Maxie looked at Shanon and Amy. "I'm not sure what Palmer's special research project is all about," she said, "but it sounds like she's pulling for an A-plus in Rain Blackburn."

Over the weekend, Shanon finally found a few minutes to dash off a quick note to Mars. She purposely kept the tone as casual as his.

Dear Mars,

Thanks for your letter. Japanese sounds like fun. So does your junk-food journey. Keeping up my Lois Lane reputation, I have some big news. A guy from Pewter is coming to live at Alma and I'll be videotaping his entire stay for a special journalism project. I can hardly wait to meet him.

16

*I hope he's not a nerd, but even if he is, it should be fun to
film him here. I'll let you know how it goes. Bye for now,*
Your pal,
Shanon

As Shanon signed her name and sealed the letter, she
thought about how easy it was to keep up her friendship
with Mars when they were only writing to each other. It
wouldn't be at all the same with Fenimore Hudson. She
would be seeing him face-to-face, every day, all day long.
The idea was scary but exciting, too.

Shanon liked the sound of his letter—friendly, smart,
cool. He didn't have to look like Tom Cruise, but she
hoped he was at least kind of cute. In any case, the pros-
pect of meeting Fen Hudson in person seemed a lot more
exciting than writing to Mars Martinez.

CHAPTER THREE

"Kate, get over here! You've got to see this!" Shanon called as she leaned out the window in the *Ledger* office. A genuine historic event was happening in a courtyard of the Alma Stephens School for Girls and she didn't want to be the only witness.

"Calm down, Shanon. I'll read your article in a minute," Kate Majors replied without even glancing up from her work. "I'm still proofreading the sports page."

"Kate!" Shanon's voice was uncharacteristically shrill. She felt a sudden urge to drag the newspaper editor over to the window by the collar of her preppie pink sweater. "He's here! It's Fenimore Hudson!"

The news of Fenimore Hudson's visit had spread across the Alma campus like wildfire. By Monday morning the entire school was eagerly awaiting his arrival.

"Fenimore! Why didn't you say so!" Kate was instantly alert. "Where?" she cried, running to the window. "I don't see anybody."

"Right there!" Shanon pointed below to a boy sitting astride a motorbike. As he kicked down the stand, hopped off, and removed his helmet, the girls could see that he was tall and broad-shouldered, with thick, sandy hair.

"*That's* Fenimore Hudson?" Kate cried. "Are you sure?"

Shanon couldn't quite believe it either. In his faded jeans and worn, brown leather jacket, he was as far removed from Shanon's nerd nightmare as a guy could get.

"Who else could it be?" Shanon replied, taking in the red duffel bag tied to the back of his bike and emblazoned with the Pewter School crest.

"The lead singer of a rock band, lost on the back roads of New Hampshire?" Kate asked, grinning delightedly.

"It's got to be him. Look at his luggage," Shanon said, pointing out the window.

But when the two girls looked outside again, the boy was gone.

"He's disappeared," Kate wailed.

"Maybe we only imagined him—like seeing a mirage of a soda machine in a desert." Shanon giggled.

But before Kate could answer, a sharp knock sounded and the office door swung open.

"Hello? Anybody home?" a deep, confident *male* voice inquired.

The girls turned to see that the motorcycle rider was no mirage. He stood in the doorway, his shiny black helmet under one arm, his red duffel bag slung over his shoulder.

"We're here!" Kate replied excitedly. She pushed her glasses higher and smoothed out her hair. "I mean, this is the *Ledger* office," she said in a calmer, more official voice. "May I help you?"

"Hi, I'm Fen Hudson, from Pewter. I'm going to be visiting Alma for a few weeks," he said with a wide, friendly smile that included both girls. Shanon had already decided he was a hunk, but that smile put him right into the super-hunk category. "I'm trying to find someone who works on the paper," he went on. "Maybe you know her—Shanon Davis?"

"That's me," Shanon piped up in a voice that came out much squeakier than usual.

"*You're* Shanon? Hey, this is great!" He quickly walked over and shook Shanon's hand. Shanon felt her face flush as she looked up at him, totally at a loss for words.

"Welcome to our school," she managed finally, thinking she sounded like a totally unoriginal dork! Fen, however, didn't seem to think so.

"You were first on my list of people to meet here," he told her. "Right after I checked in at Fox Hall. But I'm so terrible with directions," he confessed sheepishly, "I got lost and ended up here. But here *you* are, so that worked out pretty well, right?"

"Uh, right," Shanon had to agree. "You're going to live at Fox Hall?"

He looked even better close up, she thought, if that was possible. He had the most amazing smile, and his eyes were a truly awesome blue-green that contrasted perfectly with his sandy hair and dark blue T-shirt.

"That's what I've been told. Is it a good dorm?"

"It's definitely the best one *now*," Kate said so quietly that only Shanon could hear her.

"It's great. *We* both live there," Shanon said, waving her hand in Kate's direction. For a moment she'd almost forgotten there was anyone else in the room.

"Hi, Fen. I'm Kate Majors. I'm the editor here," Kate said, introducing herself. Kate, who was always painfully shy with boys, was fairly beaming at Fen, Shanon noticed.

"Nice to meet you, Kate," Fenimore said, shaking her hand. "I've read some of your articles. Pretty good stuff," he said approvingly.

Shanon had rarely seen Kate blush, but Fen's compliment brought a warm, rosy glow to her somewhat sallow cheeks. "Gee, th-thanks," she stammered.

"Hey, this is a terrific office," he said, glancing around. "You even have a fax machine?"

"We just got it," Kate said proudly. "Now we can receive or send documents almost instantly, practically anywhere."

"That's cool. We just got one at *The Bugle*, but I haven't gotten to use it yet," he said, smiling at both of them again, his beautiful blue eyes twinkling, it seemed to Shanon, especially at her.

"I'd like to interview you for our next issue, Fen," Kate said. "Your visit is big news at Alma."

"If you say so." Fen laughed shyly. So terrific and so modest—a rare combination for most boys, Shanon thought. "Figured out a good headline yet?" he asked Kate in a teasing tone.

PEWTER GUY TURNS OUT TO BE FEN-TASTIC! was the first thought that came to Shanon's mind.

"I'll think of something," Kate replied.

"Well, we can talk anytime you're free," Fen said breezily. "I'll look for you later at the dorm, Kate," he promised. "But now I'd better be getting over there. If one of you ladies would be kind enough to point me in the right direction. . . ."

"I can point you—I mean *show* you where it is," Shanon volunteered. "I have to be getting back to Fox Hall now anyway."

21

"Why don't we go over there and I'll check into my room. Then you can tell me all about your project."

"I have some notes I can show you," Shanon said. Fen's easy charm was taking her by storm. She'd never met a boy who seemed so relaxed around girls and so sure of himself in a strange environment. It was hard to believe he was the newcomer at Alma, Shanon thought. If anything, it felt the other way around.

Fen swung his duffel bag up over his shoulder and said good-bye to Kate. Then he and Shanon walked out to the courtyard. Shanon had forgotten all about his motorcycle, but there it was. He secured his duffel on the back again and hopped on, starting up the motor with a roar.

"Ever ride on one of these, Shanon?" he asked over the roar.

"Uh—no," Shanon shouted back nervously.

"You'll love it," he predicted. "Just hop on." He slid up on the seat to make room for her. Not a lot of room, but enough. Shanon took a deep breath and climbed aboard.

"Here we go." Fen put the bike in gear and gunned the gas. "Hang on tight now," he yelled.

The bike pulled away from the courtyard with a lurch, and Shanon grabbed on to Fen. Riding on a motorcycle was like nothing Shanon had ever experienced before, except for some wild ride in an amusement park. But even that wasn't quite the same.

The wind whipped her hair around her face as the quiet Alma campus passed by in a blur of spring colors. Shanon felt so wonderfully free, as if she were flying. The faster they went, the tighter she clung to Fen. Every cluster of girls they passed turned to watch them zip by; some even pointed. With her arms around Fen's waist and her cheek pressed to his leather jacket, Shanon felt like someone in a dream. "This is incredible," she screamed into the wind. Fen screamed something back, but she couldn't quite make out the words.

Shanon wished the ride would never end, but all too soon Fen pulled up to the dorm and cut the engine. He slipped off the bike, then helped Shanon dismount.

"So, how did you like it?" he asked, his hands resting on her shoulders. "Were you scared? I hope I didn't go too fast."

"Scared? No, not at all. . . ." Shanon stared up at him, feeling a little dazed. She couldn't tell if it was the effect of the motorbike ride or Fen's deep-sea eyes. "That was so wonderful! Perfect!" she said finally.

"Glad you liked it," Fen said with a grin. And slipping his arm around her shoulder, he gave Shanon a friendly little hug. "Well, you distracted your chauffeur a little with all that gorgeous long hair flying around. I'd love to take you for a really long ride sometime, but we'll have to get you a helmet, okay?"

"Uh, sure," she said. "Anytime." Shanon felt her knees turn to gelatin. Was he asking her out on a date already? They'd only met a few minutes ago, she reminded herself as they entered Fox Hall. They lingered in the hall awhile, while Shanon briefly described her project. Then ignoring the curious stares of the other girls in the dorm, she showed Fen where to get his room key.

"I guess it worked out well that we're in the same dorm," Fen said, "since we'll be working on your video so much. This will give us a chance to really get to know each other," he added, flashing Shanon another adorable grin as they finally parted company in the Fox Hall common room.

23

"I guess so." Shanon smiled back at him. She could hardly believe that she had worried about him being a nerd. She couldn't wait for her suitemates to meet him. "See you later," she added, trying to sound as cool as he did.

As for getting to know each other better, Shanon quickly decided she wanted to know every last detail about Fen Hudson.

That night, Shanon ended a very exciting day by writing a letter to her former roommate, Lisa McGreevy. Lisa had gone back home to Pennsylvania after just one year at Alma when her parents decided to divorce, and Maxie had taken her place in the suite. Even though Shanon thought Maxie was terrific, she still missed Lisa. She hoped her old roommate would eventually come back to Alma. Meanwhile, they wrote to each other often.

Dear Lisa,

I have loads of news for you. Remember how worried I was about my video-journalism project? Well, guess what? I came up with a great idea, one that qualifies as a genuine stroke of genius. A boy from Pewter is visiting Alma to write an article for his school newspaper, The Bugle, *comparing the two schools, and I am making a video of his visit! His name is Fen (short for Fenimore) Hudson, and now you are probably thinking the same thing that had Maxie, Amy, and Palmer teasing me all last week. But guess what? He showed up today and he is definitely no dweeb. They were all practically drooling when they saw me ride up to Fox Hall on the back of his motorbike. They were watching from the window—along with half the dorm! They are out of control about Fen and have had to* admit they were wrong for teasing me so much. (Palmer even offered to help carry my video equipment around campus just to get near him!) But he's also a really neat person. He's super-smart and gave me lots of terrific ideas for the video. He also told me that he could tell I was really bright from my letter, but he never expected I'd be so cute! Can you believe he actually said that to me?

Mars always says I'm smart, but he never calls me cute or pretty or anything like that. Anyway, write back soon! I really miss you.

Love,
Shanon

CHAPTER FOUR

"What about this one," Maxie said to Amy: "If you were on a desert island and could only bring two books, what would they be?"

"Books? What about tapes or CDs?" Amy said. "I would bring Paula Abdul and Mean Streak."

"I would bring Fine Young Cannibals and Vivaldi's *Four Seasons*," Maxie offered. "But the idea isn't to figure out what *we* like," she said. "It's to figure out what Paul and Nikos like."

Since Amy and Maxie both had new pen pals, they had decided to make up a questionnaire to find out more about the boys. The girls in 3-D had made one up last year for their original pen pals, but Maxie had decided it could definitely be improved upon.

"I don't know if Nikos reads much," Amy said with a shrug. She strummed her guitar, then adjusted one of the strings. "Questions and answers," she sang to an improvised tune. "A scream in the dark. Liars and dreamers. The truth is a bark. . . ."

"A bark? Like a dog bark?" Palmer, who was sitting on

her bed reading a fashion magazine, suddenly looked up. "What's that supposed to mean?"

"Bark as in a sailing ship," Amy informed her. "Didn't you read your Shakespeare for Mr. Griffith's English class tomorrow? There's going to be a quiz."

"I'll get to it." Palmer sighed, turning back to her magazine. Palmer's mother had promised her a shopping trip to New York when school ended—*if* Palmer got some decent grades. Unfortunately, right now, all Palmer wanted to study up on were the latest styles.

"How about this?" Amy asked, bursting into song again: "Questions and answers. The hoot of an owl. Liars and dreamers. The truth is a howl—"

"I like that better than bark," Maxie broke in. "But can't we finish this questionnaire now and work on your song later?"

"Oh, right. Sorry," Amy put her guitar down and devoted her complete attention to Maxie. "What do we have so far?"

" 'What is your greatest dream? What is your worst nightmare?' and the question I just read about the books— or tapes," Maxie added.

"How about, 'Do you believe Earth has been visited by aliens from other planets?' "

"That's dumb," Palmer said from behind her magazine. "They'll think you're really juvenile."

"I don't think it's a dumb question at all," Amy said slyly. "I think some people actually have roommates from other planets. But they're afraid to cause a panic by telling everyone about it."

Her roommate's teasing tone brought Palmer out from behind her magazine again. "I think sending Paul and Nikos questionnaires to fill in about themselves is sort of . . . dweeby. They probably won't even fill them out."

"You didn't always think it was dweeby, Palmer," Amy reminded her. "You've sent a questionnaire to all of your pen pals so far, except for Rain."

"That's because all of my pen pals, except Rain, were very immature." Palmer flipped back a strand of her long blond hair. "I would *never* send one to Rain. Not in a zillion years."

"You really think it's dumb?" Maxie asked hesitantly. This whole business of having a boy pen pal was new territory for her. She didn't want to make a big mistake and have Paul think *she* was a dweeb.

"Don't listen to her, Max," Amy said. "The only reason she isn't sending Rain a questionnaire is because this time she has you."

"I don't know what you're talking about," Palmer said, glaring at Amy.

"What do you mean?" Maxie asked, confused. "What do I have to do with it?"

"Palmer doesn't need to send Rain a list of questions because she's been asking *you* all about him for weeks. Then she goes and looks things up in the library. That's why she can say it's silly," Amy explained.

"That's not true," Palmer protested.

"Oh, really? I've heard you ask Max about the kinds of foods he eats, what kind of car he likes, where he goes for vacations, where he buys his clothes, what brand of sneakers he wears. . . ." Amy sounded as if she could have gone on forever.

"Okay, so I asked Max a few questions about Rain. He *is* her cousin," Palmer said, defending herself.

28

Now that Amy mentioned it, Maxie realized Palmer *had* been working Rain's name into their conversations a lot lately.

"I don't mind talking about Rain," she told Palmer with a shrug. "But even though we were very close when we were little kids, I hardly see him anymore. I'm not sure my information is going to help you much."

"Don't be silly, Max," Palmer said smoothly. "I don't talk to you about Rain just to get information on him! No matter *what* Amy thinks," she added, making a face at her roommate.

"Come on, Palmer. If you didn't have Maxie here to answer your questions, you'd be helping us write this questionnaire, right?" Amy prodded her.

"Well . . . I wouldn't go that far," Palmer said, tossing the magazine aside. "But if it was up to me, I certainly wouldn't include that question about aliens. That one is *too* dumb."

"I sort of like it," Maxie said. "Let's add, 'Would you like to meet a space alien? And if you did, what would you ask it first?' "

"That's cool," Amy agreed. "But first I think we need to ask the basic stuff—like where they grew up, if they have any sisters, brothers, or pets. You know."

"Right," Maxie said, making more notes. "How about something a little juicier as well—like 'Did you ever go steady with a girl?' "

"Great!" Amy sat up, suddenly more interested. "I would also want to know who, when, and for how long."

"You really want all the dirt, don't you?" Maxie giggled as she copied down Amy's suggestion.

"Not quite. If we really wanted *all* the dirt, we could

ask, 'Did you ever kiss a girl? Who, when, and for how long?' " Amy replied mischievously.

"Amy! We can't ask them that!" Maxie gasped.

"Okay, maybe that is going a *little* too far," Amy said agreeably. "How about a fill-in-the-blank, like 'The first thing I notice about a girl is . . . blank'?"

"I love it," Max replied. "And how about, 'What annoys me most about some girls is . . . blank'?"

"That's good, too, but I'm not sure I really want to know," Amy said with a grin. "What if Nikos says something like 'What annoys me most about some girls is that they ask too many personal questions'?"

"I don't think we asked *too* many personal questions," Maxie replied. "How can you get to know a person if you don't ask some personal questions?"

"Maybe we could be a little less obvious about it," Amy suggested. "Like ask something personal that doesn't really sound personal."

"What do you mean?" Max asked.

"Like asking, 'If you were a color, what color would you be?' If Nikos said he'd be purple, that would tell me a lot about him. But he wouldn't think it was too personal. See what I mean?"

"Sure, I get it," Maxie said. "We can ask what sort of animal they would be, or what sort of . . . food, too. How's that?"

"Perfect." Amy nodded. "Actually, that's the kind of stuff we asked on last year's questionnaire. What I'd really like to know is who Nikos's favorite female celebrity is. I hope he likes girls with dark hair," she confessed. "Maybe someone who even plays the guitar."

30

"I'll bet he does, even if she's not exactly famous yet," Maxie teased.

"Yeah . . . well, we'll see," Amy said, looking pleased and embarrassed at the same time. "I think we have enough now, don't you?"

"I think so," Maxie said, looking over her list. "I'm going to send this out right now, before I lose my nerve."

"Me, too," Amy said. "I can't wait to get Nikos's answers. Especially to our 'who-when-and-how-long' question."

Maxie and Amy quickly wrote their pen pals letters to go with the questionnaire. At the last minute, Amy added the few lines of lyrics she'd just made up at the bottom of her letter to Nikos. She decided to call the song "Fill in the Blanks," and she had a feeling Nikos might like it.

> *"Fill in the Blanks"*
> *Questions and answers,*
> *the scream of an owl,*
> *Liars and dreamers,*
> *the truth is a howl.*
> *Questions and answers,*
> *the song of a lark,*
> *Liars and dreamers,*
> *alone in the dark.*

While Amy and Max quietly wrote their letters, Palmer daydreamed about her upcoming visit to New York. She imagined herself strolling down Fifth Avenue and trying on the most terrific outfits in the exclusive—and expensive— designer boutiques.

In the fantasy, her mother was letting her buy whatever she liked. Not once did she say, "Sorry, honey. I think that leather outfit is too sophisticated for you," or "Palmer, dear, that dress is simply too short!" or "A silver lamé top? Do you really think you need it?"

After a splendid day of shopping, Palmer imagined a dream date with Rain. He took her to the most romantic restaurant for dinner and then to some really hip clubs where they danced—fabulously dressed!—the night away. Rain told her she was the most wonderful girl he'd ever met and that he was a jerk for not noticing sooner that they were a perfect match.

Her lovely daydream so lifted Palmer's spirits that she decided to write Rain another letter.

Dear Rain,

I really loved hearing all about your trip to California. Working on a movie set sounds exciting. Did you see any stars? I love the movies. I've sometimes even thought of becoming an actress, but don't tell anyone. It's sort of a secret. I am bi-coastal, too. My father lives in California, with his new wife, so I am there during vacations all the time. Maybe we can meet out there and I'll take you for a drive through Hollywood in my dad's red Lambordini. I love the shops on Rodeo Drive, don't you?

New Hampshire is so boring compared to exciting places like Los Angeles and New York. It's awful being trapped up here at Alma with no one to talk to who really has the same interests or tastes as I do. Nobody here knows anything about jazz or art, or anything, and the boys at the nearby prep schools are such babies! I am trying to get my parents to send me to school in New York, but for now I will have to be content with just a visit. My mother promised to take me shopping there when school is finished. I love Fifth Avenue—especially Gucci and Fendi. They have all the hippest styles.

I also bought a ton of tapes and CDs last time I was in New York. I found some terrific Gershwin CDs I couldn't resist. I'm listening to one right now—"Blues Rhapsody." Got to go now. Hope to hear from you soon.

Your friend,
Palmer

CHAPTER FIVE

"Hey, watch where you're going!"

Barely able to see around her video equipment and books, Shanon collided with Georgette Durand, Palmer's stepsister, as she entered the dining room. Shanon nearly knocked Georgette's breakfast all over her gorgeous outfit, but the younger girl caught her tray just in time.

"Sorry," Shanon apologized with an awkward smile.

"If you're looking for Fen Hudson," Georgette said, "he's sitting over there, by the window."

"Thanks, I see him now."

Fen had only been on campus a few days, but it seemed that everybody at Alma knew him already. They also knew that Shanon was practically his shadow as she followed him faithfully around campus with her video camera. She and Fen had agreed to meet this morning, under the clock tower. But after waiting there for almost half an hour, Shanon finally assumed she'd misunderstood the plan and went looking for him elsewhere.

And there he was—sitting at a large table, surrounded by an interested audience. Shanon had hoped to get some footage of him starting the day with a typical Alma Stephens breakfast. But this looked like an early meeting of the Fen Hudson Fan Club.

When Fen saw her coming he waved. "Hey, Shanon. How are you doing?"

"Hi, Fen." Shanon made her way through the crowd and sat down next to him. "I was supposed to film you eating breakfast this morning. Remember?"

"Oh, right! What an airhead I am sometimes!" Fen smacked his forehead. "I forgot. Sorry, pal," he said with a crooked smile. "You're not mad, are you? How about if we do it later? I'll eat bran flakes for lunch. Yummy!"

Shanon laughed at Fen's silly apology. It wasn't such a big deal after all. There'd be plenty of other chances to film him at breakfast, and she was sure he hadn't stood her up intentionally. He obviously had a lot on his mind. And not only her video—which he could have just refused to do, she reminded herself. Besides, he was such a sweet guy, it was hard to stay mad at him for long.

"No . . . I'm not mad," she said. "We can do it another day."

"You're the best, Shaney." He put his arm around her shoulder and gave it a little squeeze. "Wish I could hang out for a while, but I've got to get over to French."

"I have a class, too," Shanon said. "But you won't forget about the phys. ed. footage I want to get this afternoon, will you?" she said, reminding him again of the shooting schedule they'd worked out the day before.

"I wouldn't miss it for anything," Fen said. "And you're going to do an interview segment after, right?"

"Right," Shanon said happily.

"You're the boss," he said, whipping his hair from his

eyes and flashing another adorable grin at her. "But are you really going to make me eat bran flakes for lunch?" he asked in a plaintive but totally cute way.

"Of course not, silly!" Shanon giggled, along with the other girls at the table who had been listening in on their conversation.

"That's cool," Fen said, sweeping up his knapsack. "As you know, your slightest wish is my command," he added, sounding almost—but not quite—serious. "Catch you later."

Shanon quickly lifted the video camera to her shoulder and zoomed in on Fen, capturing his exit from the dining hall. He waved to the girls at the table and they all waved back.

Getting to know Fen had changed Shanon's life in only a few short days. For the very first time, she felt she knew what all those gooey love-song lyrics and romantic movie scenes were really about. It was scary to admit it, even to herself, but she thought she was truly falling for Fen. All he had to do was look at her in that special way of his and she went sailing off into outer space. The best part was that she was almost positive he felt the same way about her. He was always hugging her and kissing her cheek for no reason at all, and he seemed to love touching her hair and teasing her. He'd even made up a cute nickname for her—Shaney. No other boy had ever treated her the way Fen did. It was just perfect.

Later that day, Shanon filmed Fen playing softball in phys. ed. The girls in his class were tough competitors, and Fen had to play hard to keep up. He belted out a sharp line drive in the second inning, but was tagged out in a neatly turned double play.

Later, he waved off the other girls when an easy, high fly was hit his way, yelling, "I've got it! I've got it!" But at the last minute, he slipped on the grass, landing squarely on his bottom, and fumbled the catch. When the other team scored an extra run on the play, Shanon could see that some of Fen's teammates were annoyed. As a good reporter, she felt obliged to catch the entire episode on film, even though it wasn't very flattering to her subject.

After the softball game, Fen met her in front of the gym. They had planned to film the interview segment in the Fox Hall common room, but Fen thought it would be more fun to do it outside.

"It's such a beautiful afternoon. Why don't we take a walk along the river instead?" he suggested.

"Great!" Shanon said. Since Fen's first day at Alma, they'd hardly spent any time talking alone. It seemed that she was either filming him (brushing his teeth, walking to classes, attending a dorm tea) or he was surrounded by other girls. She was eager for a chance to get some really personal material about Fen without a lot of interruptions.

They walked across the quad in silence, then found a shady spot by the riverbank and sat down.

Shanon set the camera up on a tripod and turned it on. "I'm going to ask you a few questions about yourself and just let the camera run, okay?"

"Sure," Fen said. He had showered after the game and his wet hair was slicked back and gleaming, accentuating the sharp planes of his handsome face. Leaning against a tree trunk, with his arms looped around his knees, Fen seemed totally relaxed in front of the camera. Totally relaxed, and totally cute, Shanon couldn't help noticing.

After Fen told her that he had grown up in Greenwich,

Connecticut, that his father was an attorney and his mother taught archaeology at Yale, Shanon asked, "How long have you been at Pewter?"

"Two years," he replied. "Before that I went to a day school in Connecticut. I like Pewter. It's a good school. Better than some others I've been to. But comparing Alma and Pewter, I guess I could say that the best thing about Alma is the worst thing about Pewter."

"What do you mean?" Shanon asked.

"There are no girls at Pewter," he replied with a grin. "But Alma is loaded with them."

"I hope that's not the only thing you like about Alma," Shanon said, leaning back so she was out of camera range. She could feel herself blushing whenever Fen made one of his teasing, provocative remarks. But the whole world didn't have to see how he affected her. Fen Hudson had to be the cutest guy in the world, no doubt about it.

"I like a lot of other things, too," he assured her. "I do miss working on *The Bugle*, though. But I just saw last week's issue and they don't seem to be missing me much."

Shanon had to laugh at his woebegone expression. "Maybe they do more than you think," she said. "Do you like your *Bugle* work enough to pursue a career in journalism?"

"Absolutely," Fen said. "My father wants me to be a lawyer, like he is, but that just isn't my thing. I think I've always wanted to be a reporter, ever since I was a kid. How about you?"

"Me, too," Shanon said. "When I was real little I even had a make-believe newspaper with my friends. We called it *The Daily Pineapple*," she admitted, giggling at the silly name. "I guess it was a combination of *The Daily Planet* from *Superman* and the name of our street, Pineapple Street, in Brighton."

"You're from Brighton?" Fen sounded surprised.

"My dad owns a service station and store in town. I work there sometimes in the summer," Shanon said proudly. "I guess you'd say we're a pretty close family. My grandmother and aunts and uncles live nearby, and we see them a lot. My family has always lived in this part of New Hampshire. So far, I'm the only one who's gone to Alma. I was lucky enough to win a scholarship."

"I knew you were smart, Shaney, but you must be a real genius to be here on scholarship," Fen said appreciatively.

"Hardly," Shanon protested.

"Well, I bet your family is really proud," Fen said, looking at her with a serious expression. "I guess I pictured you coming from someplace else. You know, like Greenwich or Long Island."

Shanon knew he meant from a wealthier family, not one that lived in Brighton and ran a service station. But somehow she didn't feel as if Fen was looking down on her. If anything, his attitude seemed to be one of admiration.

"Sure, they're proud, I guess," Shanon said shyly. "I'm proud of them, too."

"It must be hard for you, though," he said. "Living in two different worlds, I mean. Alma is full of rich kids and can be sort of a snooty place and then you go home on vacations to Brighton. That must be tough."

"It's not really tough," Shanon replied in a thoughtful tone, "just different, I guess."

Coming from anyone else, Fen's comment might have hurt Shanon's feelings. But Fen was so sensitive and understanding. He was the first boy who really seemed able

39

to put himself in her place and try to imagine how she might be feeling about her life. That meant a lot to Shanon. More than his good looks or clever jokes.

"You're different, Shaney," Fen said, turning his dazzling smile on her. "You are definitely the most unusual girl I've met in ages."

Shanon could feel her face turning pink with pleasure. She could hardly meet Fen's blue-green gaze.

"Hey, wait a second," Shanon said. "I'm supposed to be interviewing you! Remember?"

"Well, I'm pretty boring, being an only child and all. And a dumb one at that. No scholarships to report. In fact, I'm such a problem child my parents have to pay *extra* to keep me locked up at Pewter," he said, lowering his voice confidentially.

"That's not true!" Shanon replied with a laugh.

"That's what you think," he said. "Besides, it's much more fun asking you questions," he added with a playful tug on her long sandy hair. "I'm sure you're extremely photogenic, too. Especially when you blush like that."

"Blush like what?" Shanon replied.

"Like, for example, when I ask if you have any boyfriends pining away for you in Brighton at this very minute?"

"No!" Shanon said, blushing even more furiously. A thought of Mars flashed through her mind in a millisecond, but she decided he wasn't really a boyfriend. "Well, not—"

"Like that, I mean," Fen said with a laugh. "That was a beauty."

"Well, we'll never know because I'm cutting out all that stuff about me," Shanon said with a laugh.

"What a waste," Fen said, looking up at her from where

he had stretched out on the grass, his muscular arms folded under his head. "Maybe I'll make a video about *you* next semester. Of course, you'd have to come visit Pewter."

"Maybe I will," Shanon said lightly. Inside, though, her heart was racing. Fen really made her feel special. He must like her as much as she liked him. Why else would he say such things? She didn't know quite what it was about Fen, but she had never met a boy who was so easy to talk to and joke around with. Not even Mars. Fen was so witty and smart. He knew about everything—art, music, books, politics. When they were together talking, time just flew by.

"I guess we can finish this some other time," Shanon said, glancing at her watch. She got up and gathered her belongings, but didn't turn off the camera yet. "How do you like your classes so far?"

"The classes here are really good, and the teachers are great. They sure do pile on the work, though." Fen groaned. "I've got to hustle to keep up. I've been staked out in the library almost every single night since I got here."

"I have some work to do in the library tonight, too," Shanon said. "Maybe I'll see you there."

"Why don't we go over together?" Fen suggested. "I can meet you in front of the dorm after dinner."

"Sure," Shanon agreed with a smile. She would not only be able to get some good shots of Fen hard at work in the library, she'd get to study with Alma's hottest "celebrity" student.

Shanon hurried back to Fox Hall and found her suitemates waiting for her to go to dinner. Since Fenimore had arrived, she'd barely spent any free time with them.

"Sorry I'm late, guys. I was just hanging out with—"

"We know. Fen Handsome—I mean *Hudson*," Maxie said knowingly.

"Gosh, in the entire history of Alma only one boy ever visited for longer than two hours, and not only is he too cute to be believed but our very own suitemate gets to spend every spare second with him!" Amy exclaimed. "What luck!"

"It's not luck. It's my assignment," Shanon said firmly.

"Everybody thinks you guys are dating," Maxie said.

"Who said that?" Shanon gasped. "It's not like that."

"But Fen really likes you," Maxie persisted. "Anybody can see that."

"And you really like him," Amy added. "So maybe it's more 'like that' than you think."

"Come on, guys. I guess we do like each other. But I *am* making a video and this *is* hard work. You wouldn't believe how heavy that camera gets."

"It's a good thing Fen is so big and strong," Maxie quipped. "And gallant enough to carry it around *for* you."

Shanon knew they had her there. It was true. Fen had been helping her with the camera a lot.

"And you and Fen looked pretty cozy talking under the trees by the river this afternoon," Amy said. "I passed the two of you walking back after gym. I waved, but you didn't even notice. It sure looked like a date to me," she concluded.

"It was an interview!" Shanon protested. "The camera was running the whole time . . . practically."

"Shanon, lighten up," Palmer advised, squeezing her friend's shoulder. "So what if you and Fen like each other? If you *didn't* have a major crush on him, I think we'd have to take you over to the infirmary. Every girl at Alma wishes she were in your shoes. If I were you, I'd just relax and enjoy it!"

"I'm only doing the assignment," Shanon insisted. "But I do really like Fen. He's just . . . well, wonderful."

"Fen *is* pretty neat," Maxie agreed. "But what about Mars?"

"Mars is still my pen pal," Shanon replied, sounding a bit guilty even to her own ears. "Nothing's changed between us." But the truth was, she'd barely given Mars a thought all week.

"Mars is miles away at Ardsley, but Fen is right here in Fox Hall," Amy piped up. "It's no crime to like two guys at once."

"Especially when one in particular seems to really like you so much, too," Palmer said.

"What do you think, Max?" Shanon asked her roommate.

"I can't imagine liking two guys at once. I'm having enough trouble with just one," Maxie said honestly.

"What Mars doesn't know won't hurt him," Palmer assured Shanon.

"I don't know about that," Amy said. "But what's hurting me right now is my stomach—I'm starving! Let's get over to the dining hall before they run out of food."

Palmer had the right idea, Shanon told herself as the four Foxes walked over to the dining hall. There was no need to worry about Mars; she should relax and enjoy the time she spent with Fen. She was glad she'd talked things over with her friends. They always helped her feel better.

Shanon decided she would write to Mars after dinner, but she had to go with Fen to the library. *I'll write to him tomorrow*, Shanon promised herself, *when I can concen-*

trate better. It was hard to think of anything but the wonderful afternoon she had spent with Fen. She pictured herself on a wild motorcycle ride with Fen, her arms looped around his waist, the wind whipping through her hair, and the fabulous feeling that they were almost flying.

The only thing more exciting than daydreaming about Fen was the fact that she was seeing him again in just a few short minutes.

CHAPTER SIX

Dear Maxie,

   Help! I lost my brains! As you can probably imagine, it was a real drag. All that work dissecting them and down the drain. It's tough to get a whole new set on short notice. I sent away to the lab supply house for a rush order—and then the first set turned up safe and sound in the back of the lab fridge.

   What about this Pewter guy visiting Alma? He's probably a total dork, right? I can just picture him. Or rather, imagine his scent. (We call it Pew U. for short, since that school stinks.) Poor Shanon. No offense, but I can't imagine a video about a Pew turning out well. Write soon. My brain is fried from studying so much. Lucky I have a spare.

                              Hoping to hear from you soon,
                              Paul

Dear Amy,

   I loved your letter. Your schedule sounds really packed. I don't know where you find the time to play so many sports, go to classes, study, and also write songs. If you are anywhere near as great at racing laps as you are on the softball field, the swimmers on other teams had better watch out. I don't like to swim in pools, but I do love the ocean. Down in New Orleans we were close to the Gulf beaches and the Mississippi River, of course. Have you ever been to the Big Easy (that's what we call New Orleans sometimes). If you like spicy food and great music, it's the most perfect place in the world. Whenever I go back, I go straight to the French Quarter (which is a cross between New York City's Greenwich Village, the left bank in Paris, and Disney World!). It is the most amazing place to be during Mardi Gras, when everyone is dancing in the streets and wearing wild costumes. I will show you a picture of me in my costume sometime for a laugh. Thanks for sharing your song lyrics with me. I found them very inspiring. Write soon.

Nikos

Dear Palmer,

Thanks for your note. You sound pretty excited about your shopping trip. I was into that designer-label scene for a while myself, I must admit, but I guess it's just a phase you go through at a certain age. It doesn't seem that important to me these days since I am so into my music and getting some great jobs. Sure, I'd love to cruise through Hollywood in your dad's Lamborghini (this is the way it's spelled, believe it or not) someday, but I thought you said he had a Mercedes. He must really love cars to have so many. So you really like Gershwin, too. What a coincidence. He is my favorite American composer. Or maybe you already knew that? I thought I knew all his compositions, but I've never heard of the one you mentioned,

"Blues Rhapsody." (Perhaps you meant "Rhapsody in Blue"?) Got to run. I have a gig (piano-playing job) tonight at a private party on the Upper West Side.

Best,
Rain

Dear Shanon,

Tell me more about Fenimore Hudson! He sounds great. Much more interesting than Mars—not to take anything away from your old friend. Mars is a really nice guy, but he can be a little childish. Your friend Fen, however, sounds totally awesome. I'll bet everyone else is so jealous of you they could die. (Especially Palmer. I love it!) Nothing exciting like that ever happens to me down here in Pennsylvania.

I do have one admirer at school—this really awful guy named Leonard Vitek. He's a total computer nerd and he won't leave me alone. No joke! He follows me around like a forlorn hound dog. He even looks sort of like a hound dog, which makes it kind of sad. He calls my house all the time, using lame excuses like homework assignments. I told him I have a boyfriend who goes to school in New Hampshire, but that hasn't discouraged him at all.

You can't imagine how much I miss hanging out with you guys at Alma—especially our pizza pig-outs when we all studied together. It was like a sleepover every night. Send news fast about your adventures with you-know-who. This is better than watching the soaps!

Love & hugs,
Lisa

Dear Shanon,

Sorry I didn't have time to write back right away after getting your note. I have been very busy, too. You must be hard at work on your video by now. Too bad it has to be about a guy from Pewter. They are all such slugs. I have to study for a Japanese quiz now, but I did want to send you the enclosed Emergency First-Aid Kit to help you with your video. I have a feeling you'll need it.

Don't work too hard—
Mars

When Shanon looked inside the envelope, she found a big wooden clothespin. The tag attached read: WARNING: APPLY DIRECTLY TO NOSE WHEN YOU ARE WITHIN SMELLING RANGE OF A PEW!

"Very funny, Mars!" Shanon said out loud after she read the letter. "As *usual*."

"What's the matter?" Maxie asked, putting down her letter from Paul.

"Here, take a look at this," Shanon said, handing her the crumpled-up letter and clothespin.

Maxie scanned the note, looked at the clothespin, and burst out laughing.

"It *is* pretty funny, Shanon," she said almost apologetically. She could see that her roommate was *not* amused. "I'm sure he didn't mean to make fun of your project."

"That's the problem with Mars," Shanon replied, pulling a brush through her long shiny hair. "Everything is a joke to him. He can't be serious about something for more than five seconds. And he never talks about his real feelings."

"Like Fen, you mean?" Maxie said.

"What's wrong with Fen?" Shanon replied. "He's said more nice things to me in two weeks than Mars has in almost two years."

"That's just it." Maxie shrugged. "You only met Fen two weeks ago, but you've been writing to Mars forever."

"I know it hasn't been long," Shanon admitted. "But I sometimes get the feeling that Fen and I have known each other forever. It's like he can read my mind or something."

"Actually, I don't think Mars is all that hard to read either," Maxie said. "I bet that gag was his way of telling you he does care about you."

"Come on, Max," Shanon replied with a sigh. "I know you're an expert on jokes, but I don't see much romance in a corny joke and a clothespin."

"Maybe not," Maxie said. "But some people find it easier to make a joke than to reveal their true feelings. Especially their romantic ones."

"Well, maybe I just prefer guys who can express their real feelings. Fen doesn't have to make jokes all the time. We can talk about really personal things. And he's not afraid to show me that he likes me."

"I guess you know better," Maxie said doubtfully. "But it seems awfully silly to me to trash a whole friendship over a little thing like a clothespin."

Shanon looked down at the clothespin in the palm of her hand and Mars's scrawled handwriting on the tag. She didn't know what to say. Maybe Maxie didn't quite understand. It didn't seem like such a little thing to Shanon.

CHAPTER SEVEN

"Eck!" Shanon felt a gentle tug on her ponytail and whirled around in her desk chair to find Fen grinning behind her.

"Sorry, I couldn't resist," he confessed.

"That's okay, you just startled me," Shanon said, her heart pounding. She and Kate were alone in the *Ledger* office. She had been concentrating so hard on her article that she hadn't even heard the door open.

"Pulling ponytails is a definite weakness of mine," Fen said in a serious voice. "Yours is just too totally ponytail-ish to pass up."

"Thanks . . . I think," Shanon said. Fen had a way of charming her, even after he'd just nearly scared her to death. It made her smile. She unclipped her messed-up hair and gathered it up in one bunch again.

"Working on anything interesting?" Fen asked, sitting down on Shanon's desk and idly picking up her article.

"It's about a new program of special guest speakers that will begin next fall," Shanon said. "I'm almost done with the first draft."

"Looks good," Fen said, handing it back. "Want to meet

me at the library later? I have to do some research for a debate."

"Really? What class?"

"History," Fen said. He picked up her marker and tried to balance it on the end of his index finger.

"Who are you facing?" Shanon asked him.

"Gina Hawkins. Do you know her?"

"She's really smart," Shanon replied. Gina was one of the brightest girls at Alma and a major force in the drama department. She was also very pretty and full of energy. Shanon didn't envy Fen, facing Gina in a debate. "I'd be well prepared if I were you."

"Thanks for the warning. I'll just hit the books and hope for the best, I guess," Fen said. He flipped the marker up in the air with one hand and caught it behind his back with the other.

"I think I'll film it, if Gina doesn't mind," Shanon said. In the past two weeks she'd taken lots of footage of Fen in his classes, but nothing as dramatic as a debate.

"Great, then we can see instant replays, just like on TV," Fen quipped as he hopped off the desk. "See you at the library?"

"Sure," Shanon said. "I'll meet you in the reference room."

With a wave and the special smile that made Shanon feel almost light-headed, Fen was on his way.

"It was nice of Fen to stop and say hello," Shanon said to Kate after he left. "He really seems interested in *The Ledger*. He's always giving me good story ideas."

"Maybe," Kate said, peering at Shanon over the rims of her glasses. "I think he really came by to check out the story we did on him, before it goes to the printer. See if he got good press."

Shanon didn't know what to say. Kate hadn't been very friendly to Fen, but Kate was like that sometimes—even when she really liked a person. And suddenly Kate sounded as if she didn't really like Fen anymore.

"Why do you say that?" Shanon asked.

"Just a feeling I have, that's all," Kate said.

"Fen isn't like that," Shanon said. "If he wanted to see the story he would have just asked for it. Fen is very honest and direct."

"Well, you're the expert on Fenimore Hudson, that's for sure," Kate said crisply. But Shanon had the feeling Kate still didn't agree with her.

Mr. Seganish's upper-level history class was studying the recent dramatic changes in Eastern Europe. The debate was about German reunification, with Fen presenting the pro position and Gina arguing against it. It seemed to Shanon that Fen had gotten the easier side of the argument. But when he got up to speak, she wasn't so sure. Fen's presentation was brief and vague, and Shanon felt her heart beat faster each time he stumbled over a word or idea. By contrast, Gina's presentation was full of facts and quotes and was much more convincing overall. Of course, Shanon told herself, Gina Hawkins *was* the star of the drama department. Public speaking was second nature to her.

He's just a little nervous, Shanon decided. *He'll loosen up when he gives his rebuttal.* But Fen seemed even less impressive when he got up to speak the second time. Gina, however, was at her best then, and even Shanon had to admit that she made Fen look totally out of his league.

"Thank you, Gina and Fen," Mr. Seganish said when the rebuttal period was up. "Now it's time to vote."

A student panel had been assigned to determine the winner, just like a real debate. Gina won easily, by a vote of five to two. And even though Fen didn't seem at all upset with the verdict, Shanon found herself feeling surprisingly let down. Fen had once told her he thought the classes at Alma were stimulating, and Shanon had been planning to pair that statement, which she'd recorded earlier, with this scene. But now she wasn't so sure that was a good idea. For some reason, Fen just hadn't come across very well.

"Gina really goes all out for that type of thing," she said when the class was dismissed. "I think she wants to be a lawyer. She'd make a great one."

"She wasn't bad. The topic didn't exactly inspire me, though," Fen replied with a wink. "And, of course, she knows the teacher a lot better and had a lot more time to prepare."

Shanon didn't know what to say. It had been clear to everyone that Gina's presentation was far better, especially since she had the harder side to argue. Even so, if the student panel had been playing favorites, Fen should have won hands down. Shanon gave him a sympathetic smile as she suddenly realized he might feel more embarrassed about his performance than he was willing to admit.

"I have my bike outside," Fen broke the silence. "Want to take a ride?"

"Sure, I'd love to." And Shanon forgot all about the debate in the blink of an eye.

As they roared across campus, Shanon felt wild and free. Fen was so exciting to be with. His time at Alma seemed to be going by so quickly. Her life was going to be awfully boring when he left. He was truly one in a million, and she only hoped her video would be good enough to show that.

CHAPTER EIGHT

When they reached Fox Hall, Fen slowed the bike down and came to a stop. Shanon's heart sank. The ride couldn't be over already.

"I just remembered something," Fen said. "I got hold of an extra bike helmet. I'll just run up and get it for you. Then we can go for a real ride."

"I'll come with you," Shanon offered, following him into the dorm. "I might as well change into something more comfortable."

"Okay, knock on my door when you're ready," Fen said as they parted on the stairway.

Shanon quickly slipped into a pair of new jeans and a red sweater Fen had once admired. She had been tying her hair back in a ponytail lately, ever since Fen said he liked it that way. But now she decided to wear it loose. She dabbed on some lip gloss and some of Amy's clear mascara. She didn't want Fen to think she'd run to her room just to put on makeup, but she hoped he'd notice that she looked better—without being able to quite figure out why.

"I'm ready," she said, standing in the open doorway of

Fen's room. She'd never actually been to his room before. She was dying to look around, but she didn't want to seem nosy.

"Come on in," Fen invited. "Here, try this on." He placed the yellow helmet over her head. It was way too big and came down over her eyes. They both started laughing.

"Not exactly one size fits all," Shanon said, her voice muffled from inside the helmet.

"I think you look kind of cute," Fen said, tapping the top of the helmet with his knuckles. "Do you remember that cartoon character Atom Ant?"

"Atom Ant?" Shanon laughed, pulling off the helmet. "I'm not going to go riding on your bike looking like a bug!"

"Are you kidding? You're the cutest arachnid I know," Fen teased, dropping the helmet onto her head again.

"Ants are not arachnids. Arachnids have eight legs," Shanon corrected him, pushing the helmet far up so she could at least see him.

"And definitely the smartest," he went on with a grin. "I think you're right, though. This thing is way too big for you. It might fly off and hurt somebody," he said, helping her take it off again. "Maybe we should wait on the ride. It's really not safe to go very far without one."

"Okay," Shanon said, trying to hide her disappointment. She had really been looking forward to the ride—and to being alone with him.

But once again, Fen seemed to read her mind. "Want to hear this tape my friend at Pewter sent me?" he asked, walking over to his tape deck. "It just came today. I haven't even played it yet."

"Sure. Who is it?" Shanon asked.

"Mean Streak," Fen said. "I've heard of them, but I don't have any of their tapes."

"They're pretty hot. Amy really likes them," Shanon said.

As he fiddled with the tape player, she gazed around the room and looked at his belongings. He hadn't brought that much from Pewter. There was a big poster on the wall that said, "Free South Africa Now," and a Yankee baseball cap on a bookshelf. She also noticed a picture of his family on his desk. They looked just the way Shanon had imagined them. She was relieved to see there weren't any pictures of a girl around the room.

"This is pretty good." Fen started tapping his foot to the beat of the music. "Shut the door so I can turn it up a little," he said.

Shanon got up and closed the door. As it clicked shut she felt a funny feeling in the pit of her stomach. She wondered if there was some rule at Alma about being alone with a boy in his room. Then she almost laughed out loud. How would there be such a rule when Fen was the first boy to even *have* a room on campus!

"Hey, what are you laughing at? My dancing, I bet," Fen said. He was up on his feet now, moving to the music. "I'm not exactly Michael Jackson. Come to think of it, I'm not even Bo Jackson."

"Your dancing is great," Shanon assured him. Most boys were so stiff and self-conscious when they danced, or else they got so intense about it, they looked as if they were doing warm-ups for a football game. But Fen looked just right—cool and relaxed.

"Come on, let's dance to this. It's a good song," Fen said, taking her hand.

He pushed aside the desk chair to make more room, but it was still close quarters. That was fine with Shanon. She was really having fun. She shook her head and let her hair fly all around.

"Hey, you're pretty good yourself," Fen said. "How come you never told me you liked to dance, Shaney?"

"I guess you never asked," she replied.

The next song came on and they danced to that one, too. Then a slow song came on. Shanon was ready to sit down and take a break, but before she knew what was happening, Fen took her hands and pulled her close.

"Don't sit down yet," he said. "Let's dance some more. This is fun."

"Sure," Shanon said. It *was* fun—more than she'd had in ages. Fen held her loosely with his hands at her waist and she put her hands up on his shoulders. He was so close she could barely look up at him without brushing her face against his cheek. Holding each other in the middle of his room, they swayed to the music.

"This is a pretty song," Fen said softly, his breath tickling her ear.

"It is," Shanon agreed. Being so close to Fen made it almost impossible to speak.

"I really like you, Shaney," Fen said. He leaned closer and stroked her hair with his hand.

"I really like you, too," Shanon said, resting her cheek against his shoulder and closing her eyes. This had to be the most wonderful moment of her life. She'd often dreamed of being alone with Fen like this, but she never thought it would really happen.

Then Fen suddenly stopped dancing and she lifted her head to look up at him. She wondered if anything was

59

wrong. He looked down at her, his blue-green eyes twinkling. He wasn't quite smiling, but he didn't look entirely serious either. After watching him through her camera for days on end, she'd gotten to know Fen's every expression, or so she thought. But she had never quite seen this look on his face.

Then he leaned closer and kissed her. His lips brushed hers very gently at first, then a bit harder. For a moment Shanon was taken by surprise; then she kissed him back. She liked the feeling of his strong arms around her, pulling her close. She felt her legs turn to rubber, heard her heart pounding—or was that his?

A loud, fast song suddenly came on the tape player and almost immediately someone banged on the door, saying, "Hey, Fen, turn it down. I'm trying to study."

"Okay, okay," Fen shouted through the door. He pulled away from Shanon and lowered the volume. When he turned back to her, he looked a little flustered. "I guess somebody out there doesn't have any taste in music," he said, running a hand through his hair. "You can't listen to a group like that really low. It ruins it."

"I guess so," Shanon replied, feeling like Dorothy from *The Wizard of Oz*—swept up by a tornado for a quick visit to Oz and then dumped back into Kansas again. She sat down on the bed and Fen sat beside her. He took her hand in both of his and looked down at it.

"Thanks for the dance, Shaney," he said quietly. "Maybe we can really go out dancing sometime. Someplace where we won't be banging our knees into the furniture."

"I didn't notice the furniture that much," Shanon replied honestly. Fen just smiled at her, and suddenly she felt very shy around him. Almost more nervous than the day they first met. She wondered why that should be after he had told her he liked her and even kissed her.

"I guess we'd better get out of here," Fen suggested. "Before somebody barges in and we get in trouble. If we can't go riding, I might as well do some work. Want to go to the library with me?"

"Uh . . . maybe I'll meet you there later. I think I'll just study in my room for a while," Shanon said.

Fen didn't seem at all fazed by their kiss, but Shanon needed some time alone to settle down and think over what had happened. Did this mean she was really his girl-friend now? As he walked her to her room, she waited for him to say something more—some hint that things had changed between them—but he didn't.

Of course he was older and definitely cooler about these things than the boys she knew, Shanon decided as she floated into her room on a cloud of pure bliss.

Later that week, Shanon began the long process of editing her footage. Some of the tape was wasted—shot at weird angles, out of focus, or just plain boring—and she cut that right away. Then she made a chart, listing each good scene she'd shot with a column for comments. Every frame in the video counted, and only the very best material would be included.

First she reviewed some tape of Fen acquainting himself with campus life. Shanon winced whenever Fen came on screen smiling and laughing with a group of girls, or putting his arm around somebody, as he so often did with her. Still, she'd have to show him socializing, even if it made her jealous to watch. And he really did like *her* best, Shanon reminded herself.

61

The scene at the softball game came on and Shanon laughed out loud as Fen made his blooper catch and landed on his bottom. The soundtrack of Fen shouting "I got it! I got it!" then "Ouch!" was priceless. And so was his clowning for the camera afterward.

Fen was such a good sport and he looked so good in his workout clothes. He pushed his hands through his hair and Shanon sighed out loud, glad there was nobody around to hear her.

Some tape shot in Ms. Grayson-Griffith's French class showed the students reading a play by Molière. Fen was reciting his lines very theatrically, but the pretty, dark-haired teacher kept interrupting him to correct his accent. Shanon watched the scene twice, then marked it on her list as doubtful. It was so choppy. Fen sounded a little silly, fumbling over even some really simple words and phrases. Everybody sounds like that in a language class, Shanon decided. But if you see it on a video, it looks really dumb. It wasn't Fen's fault. He sounded adorable when he spoke French. She loved it when he faked a French accent to tease her.

The debate in Mr. Seganish's history class had plenty of dramatic action, just as she'd hoped. But Fen's presentation sounded even worse compared to Gina's when Shanon heard it again on video. She didn't know what to do with this material and put a question mark beside it on her comment list.

There was some good footage from Mr. Griffith's English class taken during a discussion of Shakespeare's play *Macbeth*. In reply to one of Mr. Griffith's questions, Fen gave a very good answer about Macbeth's motivation. But then Mr. Griffith asked him to refer back to the text, and it turned out Fen had confused the passage. Shanon thought she could use the scene anyway and just cut the last part out.

When Shanon finally finished reviewing the tapes, she wasn't very happy with the way it was turning out. But she didn't exactly know why. During the shooting, she'd felt sure she was getting some great footage. Yet, looking over it now, she was very disappointed.

Shanon briefly considered the possibility that Fen was not quite as brilliant as she'd thought. Then just as quickly she rejected the idea. Fen was so smart. She knew he was, and so did everybody who met him. She just hadn't gotten him at his best. This documentary business wasn't as easy as she'd thought.

CHAPTER NINE

Dear Paul,

I hope you found your brains (your real set, I mean) in time to answer our questionnaire. I really want to know more about you.

Just for the record, Fen Hudson is no dweeb. He rides a motorcycle and he's really funny and smart. Just about every girl at Alma has a crush on him. I'm sure Shanon's video will be great.

Max

Dear Max,

I'm still working on your questionnaire—all the questions I could answer, that is. It takes time to really get to know a person. You can find out what kind of food they like, what books they read, what music they listen to, etc., but that still doesn't mean you really know them. Does this make sense to you? Awaiting your reply. . . .

Your friend,
Paul

P.S. Mars won't admit it, but I think he feels really bad

64

*because Shanon hasn't written to him lately. He was upset
to hear this Pew-ster was so cool. Is she really that busy
with her video? Could you please tell Shanon to write him?
It would mean a lot to both of us. Mars is in such a bad
mood that it's driving me crazy!*

*P.P.S. When you said "just about" every girl at Alma
has a crush on Fenimore Hudson, did you mean you do,
too?*

Amy's correspondence from Nikos came in a long brown
cardboard mailing tube. Inside was a letter and a rolled-up
sheet of drawing paper. She read the letter first:

Dear Amy,
*I think questionnaires are silly, but I will answer a few
questions from yours because I'm glad you want to know
me better. I think your song lyrics are an excellent way for
me to get to know the real Amy Ho. They are like poetry
and have given me some good ideas for paintings. You
must have a very poetic side to write them, and I'm sure
you will be a very successful musician if you follow your
dream. Please send me more of your songs. I am sending
you some of my artwork. Maybe it will inspire you, too?*
                                          Nikos
*P.S. The enclosed is sort of a portrait. Hope you like it. I
worked very hard to express my true feelings and inner
vision.*

Amy eagerly unrolled the drawing paper to find a huge
painting. It was all swirling colors, and it practically made
her dizzy to look at it. Amy liked abstract art and frequently
visited museums when she was in New York. But she hon-

65

estly didn't know what to make of Nikos's work. At the bottom she read the title, penned in a bold black script: "Amy, Cloud Dancing in Ten Thousand and One Dreams." It was supposed to be her, Amy realized. Nikos had actually painted her portrait! It was flattering—or was it?

Amy propped the painting up on her desk and tried to study it from a distance. After one long look, she decided it was upside down. Turning it over, she stared at it again. Gradually a few features came into view—a big purple eye with some yellow lashes; a curlicue of a nose that looked like a piece of overcooked noodle; another eye, lopsided on the paper and neon green; a mouth that looked like a roller skate. And a mass of magenta zigzags that she guessed must represent her hair. Either that or lightning bolts were shooting out of her head.

Amy wasn't sure whether to laugh or cry. Was that what he really thought she looked like! And after all the sweet things he'd said about her in his letters, he clearly thought she looked like a space monster!

Palmer *would* pick the worst possible moment to come back into the room. Amy made a grab for the picture as Palmer burst into the sitting room, but it was too late.

"What's that? A poster?" Palmer asked curiously.

"It's nothing," Amy lied, quickly rolling the painting up.

"Let me see," Palmer insisted. "Is this what Nikos sent you in that mailing tube?" *Leave it to Palmer to guess everybody's private business,* Amy thought. "Why can't I see it?" Palmer wheedled. "Come on, don't be so secretive," she teased, grabbing the painting away from Amy.

"Palmer, it's private!" Amy cried. But Palmer had already unrolled the painting and was examining it wide-eyed.

" 'Amy, Cloud Dancing in Ten Thousand and One Dreams,' " she read aloud in a simpering voice. "A Thousand and One Nightmares would be more like it," she said. "It's not exactly flattering, but it does bear some passing resemblance—"

"Thanks a lot!" Amy cut her off.

"Only kidding," Palmer said, handing the painting back to Amy. "You have to admit he didn't do badly with the hair," she added snidely.

"It's abstract art," Amy countered, staunchly defending the horrible painting. "But you wouldn't understand, Palmer."

"I don't know much about art," Palmer replied with a withering glance, "but I do know when something is ugly."

Amy just glared at her. But inside, she was really embarrassed by Nikos's portrait. She wouldn't dare show it to anyone else. She had an urge to tear it up and throw it away. But instead she slipped it back inside the mailing tube.

Things with Nikos had been going along so well until now. Amy knew that sooner or later she would have to write him back about the portrait, and that was going to be a problem. As her mother had once told her, "If you can't say anything nice, don't say anything at all." Right now, the only nice thing she could say about Nikos's artwork was that it could be easily hidden at the back of her closet.

CHAPTER TEN

On Saturday the four Foxes took a long bike ride together. It was a perfect spring day, and the New Hampshire countryside looked fresh and green. Beyond the school, the hilly back roads ran alongside large farms, meandering through quaint villages that boasted little more than a general store, post office, and gas station.

Shanon, who had grown up in the area, led the way. As she coasted down a steep hill, she could almost imagine herself on the back of Fen's motorbike. He had invited her to go canoeing on a nearby lake that day, but Shanon had already made plans with her suitemates. She would see Fen that night anyway. They were going to watch the Saturday-night movie on the new, big-screen TV in the common room together. It wasn't exactly a real date, Shanon reflected, but it was almost like one.

A small frown flickered across her face as Mars's image unaccountably flickered across her mind. She hadn't thought of him in days, nor had she ever replied to his infamous clothespin letter. Even Maxie had stopped asking her about him, and now Shanon felt nothing but a brief twinge of guilt on his behalf. Mars had done himself in, as far as she was concerned, with his mean little joke.

The four girls pedaled along for an hour or so before stopping to rest by the river's edge. There they unpacked the delicious picnic lunch the school cook and dietician had made for them.

"Last brownie, Palmer. I think Mrs. Butter put your name on it," said Shanon, holding out the depleted bag of goodies. Everybody had eaten at least two, except for Palmer, who hadn't tasted a crumb.

"No, thanks," Palmer said. "Those carrot sticks really filled me up."

"You can't fool us, Palmer," Amy said. "You're dieting again. What is it this time? Liquid protein shakes?"

"I am not. What a silly idea. Can't I pass up a brownie without answering a million questions?"

"Not one of *these* brownies. They are food for the gods," Maxie said. She was stretched out on the grass, her arms folded under her head, eyes closed. "I would eat it myself, but I think I'm about to sink into a chocolate coma."

"Are you feeling okay, Palmer?" Shanon asked, giving her friend a concerned look.

"Sure, I'm fine," Palmer said. "Couldn't be better."

"How come you didn't go shopping today?" Amy asked her.

"Because I wanted to come bike riding with you guys," Palmer said. "Besides, I'm sort of saving my money . . . for something special."

"Your shopping trip to New York?" Shanon asked.

"It will be a trip to New York, all right, but not the one with my mother," Palmer replied in a mysterious tone. Her three suitemates were now sitting up, completely attentive.

"So? Is that all you're going to tell us?" Amy prodded. "We'll find out sooner or later, you know."

"Then I might as well tell you about it now," Palmer said, crunching down on a carrot stick. "You're all going to have to help out a little in order for this plan to work."

"Plan? What sort of a plan?" Maxie said.

"A *brilliant* plan," Palmer replied with a gleeful smile. "What other kind would I think of?"

"Uh-oh." Amy looked at Palmer and then at the other two Foxes. "Whenever Palmer has a brilliant plan, I picture a letter from our dear headmistress going home to my parents."

"Calm down, Amy," Shanon said. "Let Palmer tell us what it is before you start imagining Miss Pryn throwing us all out of school."

"Nobody's going to get thrown out of anything. This is foolproof, I promise," Palmer exclaimed. "Just listen. Next weekend, I'm going down to New York to visit Rain. I'll take a bus on Sunday morning and get there at about six o'clock. Then I'll have dinner with Rain and take a midnight bus back to Brighton. I don't have any classes on Mondays, so I can sleep all day. Nobody but you three will ever know I'm missing."

"Holy cow—she's flipped out." Amy sighed, smacking her forehead with her hand. "It must be the lack of food. She's hallucinating."

"What about dinner Sunday night?" Maxie pointed out. "Someone is sure to notice that you're not there."

"That's where you three come in. All you have to do is say I didn't feel well and decided to go to bed early. No one will check."

"But what if they do?" Shanon said, thinking Palmer

was taking a terrific risk. The Foxes would all be in trouble if anyone found out they'd covered for her.

"But they won't," Palmer insisted. "They never do. You just have to say it in a convincing way. You just have to be cool about it."

"I don't know," Maxie said doubtfully. "Maybe it's not such a good idea."

"It's a great idea," Palmer insisted. "And I'm counting on you to help me," she wailed. "I'll die if I can't go!"

"Calm down, Palmer. We didn't say we wouldn't help you," Amy assured her. "We just want to talk it over a little. What does Rain think of this idea? Does he know you're not allowed off campus except for a real emergency?"

"Uh . . . Rain doesn't know I'm coming yet. That's the best part of the whole plan. My visit is going to be an incredible surprise."

"A surprise?" Amy gaped at her roommate. "That's the dumbest thing I ever heard. You can't surprise a guy like Rain."

"Why not?" Palmer asked innocently. "I'm going to send him a card that says be home on Sunday night at about six for a special surprise. He'll think I'm going to call, or send one of those balloon-o-grams, or something."

"What if he's waiting around for your balloon-o-gram with another girlfriend?" Amy asked. "Ever think of that?"

"I don't think he'd do that," Palmer replied. "Besides, I can handle it," she added.

"What about the bus station at midnight?" Shanon asked her. "I don't think you realize how dangerous it is. Something terrible could happen to you."

"Nothing is going to happen to me . . . except that I'll

71

get to see Rain. Which is my plan," Palmer said stubbornly.

"Why is it so important that you see him?" Amy asked. "And what makes you think he even wants to see *you*?"

"I know he'll be happy to see me once I'm actually there," Palmer said. "Besides, I just *want* to."

Palmer had been too embarrassed to show her friends Rain's last letter. All she knew was that she had to see him and correct the totally false impression her letter had given him. She stood up abruptly and brushed off her pale-blue linen slacks. "I'm sorry I even told you about it," she pouted. "I should have just left a note."

"I'm glad you told us," Shanon said. It sounded as if Palmer really meant to go through with this crazy scheme. At least now they had a week to talk her out of it.

CHAPTER ELEVEN

—————◇—————

Dear Shanon,

Is it true that you've been kidnapped by aliens? Or is that just a vicious rumor? Maybe you're too busy with your video about Feni-pew to have any contact with mere Ardies. I have been spending a lot of time lately on a new interest, too. After reading your Ledger *article about literacy volunteers, I looked into the local programs. As you probably know, the girls at Brier Hall run one with the Brighton town library. They have been very friendly and promised to give me lots of help with the training. Those girls are all so hardworking and dedicated. I think their program would be a very worthy and interesting subject for a video, too. (Maybe even more interesting than some wiseguy from Pew?) Guess that's all for now.*

Mars

"That's all for now!" Shanon snorted, reading Mars's last line aloud. "That's all *forever*, Arthur Mars Martinez!" She crumpled up his letter and threw it across her bedroom—

—at the very moment Maxie opened the bedroom door and stepped into the sitting room. The wadded-up ball of paper hit her squarely on the forehead.

"What in the world!" she said, scooting back behind the door. A moment later she peeked out again. "Hold your fire! It's only me, Max."

"Sorry! I didn't know you were there," Shanon said, feeling foolish. "It's okay—you can come out now."

"What's going on?" Max asked, plopping down on the pink loveseat.

"Oh, it's nothing really," Shanon said, picking the letter up off the floor. "I'm just mad at Mars. You won't believe the letter he just wrote me. That dumb clothespin letter was bad enough, but this is too much!" She picked up the letter, smoothed it out, and passed it to Maxie.

It took Maxie only seconds to read the short note. "Well . . . I guess he didn't have to call Fen 'Feni-pew,' " she said, trying to hide a smile. "Or mention all those great Brier girls he's meeting as a literacy volunteer."

"Or tell me that their program would be a better idea for a video than my project about Fen!" Shanon sputtered.

"He didn't exactly say that, Shanon," Max pointed out. "He only said 'maybe.' "

"I know. And that's so typical of Mars. Why can't he ever come right out and say what he really means?"

"I think he just wrote that part about the Brier girls to make you jealous," Maxie said.

"I know," Shanon said. "That's typical of him, too. And it's so immature. Fen would never do something so juvenile. I don't know what I ever saw in Mars Martinez," she told Max. "Getting to know Fen was the best thing that ever happened to me. I really don't see much point in writing to Mars anymore. We obviously don't have anything worth saying to each other. I'm going to write him a letter right now and tell him I think we should stop writing."

"Are you sure you want to do that?" Maxie said, handing the letter back to Shanon. "Mars has been a really good friend to you. And until Fen came along, you seemed to like him a lot. Maybe you should think it over a little," she suggested.

"There's nothing to think about," Shanon said quietly. "Besides, I have much too much work to waste time writing letters."

Dear Mars,

Contrary to popular rumor, I have not been kidnapped by aliens. (Maybe you have been reading the National Enquirer *too much again.) I guess since you are so busy with your volunteer work, you won't have time for a pen pal anymore. That's okay with me. I understand completely, as I have been very busy myself. So maybe this has all worked out for the best. No hard feelings, I hope.*

Good luck,
Shanon

As soon as Shanon left the room to mail her letter and meet Fen down in the common room, Maxie took her place at the desk.

Dear Paul,

Something awful just happened here. I can't believe it. Shanon broke up with Mars! He wrote her a really dumb letter about all these Brier girls he's getting to know and insulting her video project. It made her so mad she wrote back and said she didn't want to be pen pals anymore. I'm afraid she really means it. So if you thought Mars was in a bad mood before, you'd better brace yourself. He's in for a shock. Why are guys so dense sometimes?

Your pen pal,
Maxie

P.S. Did you sign up for the book talk at Alma? I will be going.

P.P.S. By the way, I don't have a crush on Fen Hudson. He's not my type at all.

CHAPTER TWELVE

Dear Nikos,

Sorry it's taken me so long to write you back, but I do have a busy schedule, as you know. I was very flattered that you painted my portrait. It's extremely interesting— very lively and colorful. I have it hanging in my room, right over my desk. Everybody keeps asking about it and about the talented artist who painted it. Thanks for such a lovely gift.

Amy

Amy felt uncomfortable lying to Nikos about his painting. But she didn't see any other way out. She knew that if he ever told her he hated her song lyrics, she would be crushed. It had been really sweet of him to send her the painting and she couldn't possibly insult him by telling him her real reaction. This was clearly one of those times when it was better to save someone's feelings with a little white lie, she decided, than bludgeon them with the truth.

Dear Amy,

   Thanks for your letter. I was wild to know what you thought of the painting. I am glad you like it so much. That means a lot to me. Thanks for the compliments, but I have a long way to go as an artist. I do have some exciting news about that painting though. The watercolor I sent you was basically a rough sketch for a more final acrylic version. The final one is sort of the same, but a few colors and shapes are changed. (Of course, the title didn't change.) Anyway, the acrylic portrait is going to be in the Ardsley literary maga-zine, Aurora! *Isn't that great? It might even be chosen for the cover. All artists need inspiration. Thanks for yours.*

                                                              Inspiredly,
                                                              Nikos

"Oh, no!" Amy gasped as she read Nikos's letter over a second time.

"What's the matter now? Did the mad artist paint an-other portrait of you in a bathing suit or something?" Palmer was sitting on her bed, touching up her toenail polish.

"Worse than that." Amy sighed, flopping down on her bed like a sack of potatoes. "That painting he did of me is going to be in the Ardsley lit mag. Maybe even on the cover!"

"Don't worry," Palmer said coolly. "No one will recog-nize you . . . maybe."

"This isn't funny, Palmer. What am I going to do?" Amy moaned.

"Just tell him you don't want your picture in the mag-azine. What's so hard about that?" Palmer stretched out her leg and admired her pearly pink toes.

"I *can't* tell him that. It would hurt his feelings," Amy replied. "He thinks that painting is great. And he thinks I think it is, too."

"Well, you can either hurt his feelings or have the entire world see that incredibly flattering picture of you."

"It's not so simple," Amy said with a sigh.

"I know what I would do," Palmer said, getting up from the bed and sitting down at her desk. She took a stamp from a small heart-shaped china dish, licked it, then very carefully pressed it onto a postcard that was sitting on her blotter. "What you need is a plan, Amy. Just figure out your plan and stick to it. It makes everything so much easier."

"Like your plan to see Rain?" Stretched out on her bed, Amy tossed aside Nikos's letter and turned to eye her roommate. Palmer hadn't mentioned her crazy scheme since the day of the bike ride, but she obviously hadn't given it up.

"Here, look at this," Palmer said, passing the postcard to Amy. "Part One of the plan. Rain will be dying of curiosity. He won't be able to resist waiting around his house Sunday night to see what's going to happen."

The card had a photo of James Dean on the front side. On the back, Palmer had written:

Hope you'll be home this Sunday from 6 P.M. to midnight. A major surprise is in the works for you. You won't want to miss it! I promise—Palmer.
P.S. Remember the Renoir card you sent me? Well, I saw this card and thought of you.

"Palmer!" Amy gasped. "You're not really going through with this, are you?"

79

"Of course I am," Palmer said coolly. "Don't even think of trying to talk me out of it."

"If we really wanted to stop you, we could tell Mr. Griffith, you know," Amy said quietly.

"But you really wouldn't do that to me, would you?" Palmer asked innocently.

Amy stared at Palmer for a second. They'd certainly had their disagreements, but Amy knew she couldn't be a traitor to her own roommate.

"I guess not," she said.

"I didn't think so," Palmer said, giving her a sweet smile before staring wistfully down at her postcard again.

Amy didn't say anything. She wouldn't let Palmer sneak off and go to New York by herself. If anything happened to her, Amy knew that she and the other Foxes would never forgive themselves.

But how in the world were they going to stop her?

CHAPTER THIRTEEN

"That was a great movie. I love Humphrey Bogart," Fen said. "I must have seen all of his films about ten times each."

"I haven't seen that many," Shanon said. "But *African Queen* is my favorite."

Now every time she saw the movie, Shanon thought, it would remind her of Fen and his last night at Alma. As they crossed the quad toward Fox Hall, Fen took her hand in his. It was a cool clear night, and Shanon looked up to see a million stars sparkling above the swaying branches of the tall fir trees. She made a secret wish on one—that she and Fen would be *officially* going out together soon. Very soon.

"You're so quiet tonight, Shaney," Fen said. "Something the matter?"

"I don't know." Shanon shrugged. "I guess it's just because it's your last night," she admitted.

"I feel a little sad, too," Fen said, squeezing her hand. "We had so much fun together. Meeting you really made my visit here much better than I expected," he said, looking down at her with his familiar smile.

"Thanks," Shanon said shyly as they stopped in front of Fox Hall. Neither of them seemed eager to go inside. "What time are you leaving tomorrow?"

"Very early. I guess we'd better say good-bye now," Fen said. He took her hands in both of his. "Don't be sad, Shaney. Now it's your turn to visit Pewter," he suggested.

"Sure, I'd like that. Then I can do my own comparison." Shanon thought he might suggest a specific time for her visit, but when he didn't she decided not to press him.

"I'll send you my article. I want you to see it first," Fen promised.

"I can't wait. I bet it will be great," Shanon replied.

"We'll see. I have plenty of material, that's for sure. Do you have any vacation plans yet?" Fen asked suddenly. "Will you be hanging around Brighton?"

"I guess so," Shanon said. "I usually work for my father."

"I might be around here, too," Fen said. "Working as a counselor at a tennis camp. Maybe we could get together then. I'll take you out on my motorcycle for a real ride."

"That would be great. But you'll have to find me a helmet that fits this time," Shanon replied with a laugh, remembering the big yellow one he had made her try on.

"Right," Fen said. "Don't worry, I'll work on it."

"As long as I don't look like Atom Ant again," Shanon said, smiling up at him, unable to hide her joy at the thought of seeing him again. Was he going to say anything more? Shanon wondered. Was he going to kiss her good-bye?

"I was only teasing you about that." Fen paused and

took a deep breath. He looked down at Shanon with a sweet smile. "Well, let's not say good-bye. It's too hard. We'll keep in touch, right?"

"Of course," Shanon promised. How could he even doubt it? She'd write to him every day if he wanted her to.

"Take care, Shaney," Fen said softly. "Write to me soon, okay?" And before Shanon could answer, he leaned down and kissed her softly. Then, with his arm around her shoulders, they walked into the dorm. Moments later they went their separate ways to their rooms.

Dear Lisa,

Thanks for your funny letter. I've read it over a few times and it's really cheered me up. It's only been three days since Fen left, but it seems very quiet around here. I really miss him. He was so sweet to me his last night. He said he might be around Brighton this summer and hinted that we would be dating. Wouldn't that be great!

Meeting Fen has been like a dream come true, but now it's back to real life. I have to get down to edit all my footage, do the narration, etc. I'm sure that watching it will make me miss Fen even more, but there's no way around that, I guess. You were right about Mars. He really is immature. I decided not to write him anymore after the last letter he wrote me. I've enclosed a copy so you can see for yourself. It's just as well. I'll be writing so much to Fen now, I probably wouldn't have enough time to be Mars's pen pal anyway. Speaking of time, I guess it's time to get back to the books. Working on my video has made me fall behind in some classes, but I'll catch up.

Write,
Shanon

As soon as she finished her letter, Shanon opened up her math text and tried to settle down to some serious studying. It wasn't long before her thoughts drifted back to Fen, though. She had hoped for a letter from him by now, but decided she was being silly. He was probably too busy getting resettled at Pewter and writing his article about Alma.

She would hold out for a few more days. After all the sweet things he had said to her on their last night together, she was sure to be hearing from him soon. But then again, maybe he expected *her* to write first. . . .

Dear Fen,

Just a quick note to say hello. Is it hard getting used to Pewter again after Alma? I am so used to carrying around my video camera that I feel as if I'm forgetting something every time I leave the dorm! It has only been a few days since you left, but it sure seems quiet around here without you. I am almost through with the Studs Terkel book. It's great! I am really learning a lot from his interviews. Thanks for loaning it to me. I plan to read more of his work after this one. Any other suggestions for my vacation reading list?

I had a great time doing the video of you and, of course, getting to know you. (Maybe even the high point of my time at Alma so far.) I will be eager to hear your thoughts about the video. I'll send you a copy of the tape as soon as I can. I am also eager to read your Bugle *article about Alma. (But maybe it is already on its way?)*

I thought this was going to be a short note, but I guess it turned out longer than I planned. (Maybe I just miss talking to you, since we spent so much time together the last few weeks.) Got to get back to my homework now. I have a ton of catching up to do!

     Shanon
      (Goddess of Overdue Homework Assignments)

P.S. Are you really planning to be around Brighton this summer? I will probably be here, too.

CHAPTER FOURTEEN

———◆———

The next Monday afternoon, Shanon returned to Suite 3-D toting an armload of books and feeling totally depressed. She still hadn't heard from Fen.

"Shanon! Is it really you?" Clutching her chest, Maxie fell backward on her bed. "We thought the Phantom of the Library had dragged you off to his secret cavern under the periodical literature room!"

"What in the world are you talking about?" Shanon asked her roommate, smiling for the first time all day.

"Didn't you ever hear the story about the mad librarian who lives beneath the library?" Maxie asked quite seriously. "I thought everybody at Alma knew *that*. You knew it, didn't you?" she asked Amy, who was curled up on the loveseat.

"Sure," Amy said. "Just like the Phantom of the Opera. Except the Phantom of the Library only nabs Alma girls who have overdue books. And we all know Shanon is too perfect to keep her books past the due date," Amy teased.

Shanon tried—unsuccessfully—to smother a giggle. Her suitemates knew her too well. She couldn't bear to bring her books back to the library even a single day late.

"And what's wrong with that?" Maxie said. "We're going to celebrate with a Monstro pizza from Figaro's. We ordered it with extra mushrooms, just for you, Shanon."

"Perfect!" Shanon flopped down next to Amy. It felt good to hang out with her friends after working so hard all week. She deserved a break. Now, if only a letter from Fen would arrive.

Shanon was just about to ask if the mail had come yet when Palmer burst into the suite. She was carrying a pile of magazines and letters.

"Major mail call for our suite today!" she announced, dumping the mail on Maxie's desk. The other girls rushed over and began rummaging through the pile.

"A postcard from Rain!" Palmer screeched, jumping up and down. She was too excited to even read it. "I can't believe he got my note so fast! Do you think he figured out the surprise?"

"There's a simple way to find out, Palmer. Why don't you just read it," Amy suggested calmly.

Everyone knew that Palmer had sent her mysterious postcard to Rain a few days ago, even though they had done their best to talk her out of it. Now they waited in suspense to hear his response.

Dear Palmer,

I'm down in sunny Mexico on a work-study program till the end of the semester. It's unbelievably beautiful. I have seen the most amazing countryside the last few days. Small villages and places tourists never go. It's the greatest! Stay in touch—

Rain

Palmer was speechless for a second, obviously in shock. "*Mexico!* He never said he was going to Mexico! Why didn't you tell me about this, Maxie?" she demanded, two red spots appearing on her cheeks.

"Calm down, Palmer," Maxie replied. "This is the first I've heard about it. I *told* you Rain and I aren't that close anymore."

"Looks like your sneak-attack plan is out," Amy observed. "It's a long bus ride from New Hampshire to Mexico."

"The nerve of some people," Palmer fumed, jamming the postcard in her pocket.

"I know you were psyched to see Rain," Max said sympathetically.

"Well, Palmer, at least we can stop worrying about your getting into trouble," Shanon said. "But I do feel bad for you."

"Here's something to cheer you up," Maxie said, handing Shanon a thick envelope. "It's from Fen Hudson!"

"He sure took his time writing, but it looks like a long letter," Shanon said. She eagerly ripped it open, flopped down on the floor, and began to read:

Hi Shanon,
It sure feels good to be back here at Pewter. I guess I missed the old place more than I realized—especially my suitemates and my work on the paper. All the guys are really curious about Alma. I've been telling them that my

88

article in The Bugle *will tell it all. I've enclosed the rough draft so you can have an early look at it. I'll be interested in your opinion. Good luck with your schoolwork, the video, your scholarship, etc. You are a bright kid. That's for sure. Keep in touch.*

Sincerely,

Fen Hudson

P.S. My summer plans are still up in the air. I might join my mother at an archaeological dig in the Greek Islands. Slightly more interesting than hanging around Brighton, wouldn't you agree?

Shanon's heart sank. Fen's letter sounded so distant. She had been sure something special was going on between them. It couldn't be over so soon—or could it? Shanon felt a momentary relief as she considered the possibility that he'd been in a hurry and didn't have time to write her a longer, more personal letter. Maybe he'd just gotten a little scared about his feelings and decided to play it cool. Lots of boys were like that, she reflected.

She quickly turned to his article. She couldn't wait to see what he had written about Alma—and, of course, about her! She had barely finished reading it when Maxie sat down beside her.

"What does Fen have to say?" Maxie asked Shanon. "I'll bet he misses us all terribly and is trying to figure out a way to register at Alma next fall."

"Not exactly," Shanon began in a quiet voice. "It doesn't sound as if he misses us at all. Not *any* of us," she added pointedly.

"Let me see," Palmer said, snatching Fen's letter from Shanon.

"You're right," Amy said, peering over Palmer's shoulder. "I can't believe it. You spent every minute with the guy for three solid weeks and he sounds as if he hardly knows you!"

"And what's this 'bright kid' business!" Palmer added. "Who does he think he is, anyway?"

"What about his article, Shanon? Is there anything in there about you?" Amy asked hopefully.

Shanon almost didn't have the heart to show them what Fen had to say about Alma, but she knew she had to be honest with her closest friends. "Here," she said, reluctantly handing the article to them. "You guys can read it yourselves."

As Palmer, Max, and Amy huddled together over Fen's article, Shanon braced herself for their reactions. Just as she expected, it wasn't long before they stopped reading and began voicing their outrage.

"That guy is unbelievable!" Amy said. "He doesn't have one good thing to say about Alma—the students, teachers, or anything within a five-mile radius of here! Listen to this," she said, reading directly from the article: " 'Unfortunately, my three-week stay at Alma Stephens was a surprising disappointment. Accustomed as I was to the challenging academic atmosphere at Pewter, I found Alma's academic temperament—in a word—anemic. The teaching staff is competent, but not nearly as stimulating as Pewter's. Of course, the tepid classroom interaction may not be entirely their fault. The all-girl student population is not nearly as serious about their studies or as intellectually competitive as students at Pewter. Or perhaps at any all-boy school—' "

"I guess his debate with Gina Hawkins somehow slipped

his mind," Palmer cut in sarcastically. "I was in a few of Fen's classes," she added, "and he didn't exactly shine!"

"I was in some classes with him, too," Max spoke up. "If he had spent the whole semester here, I doubt that he would have made honor roll. He had to work pretty hard just to keep up with our *anemic* teachers and academic standards!"

"Listen to what he says about the school facilities," Palmer cried, quickly scanning the next page. "He calls the language lab 'a charming antique' and the communications lab 'adequate but nothing to write home about.' "

"According to Fen, 'The sports program at Alma provides a great deal of fun and fresh air for students, but it will hardly get you in shape for truly competitive athletic competition,' " Amy read out loud. "He doesn't even credit our teams for doing so well against other schools!"

"Wait! You haven't heard the best part." Maxie was practically hopping up and down. "He even has the nerve to give Mrs. Butter's food a bad review. He calls her cooking 'tolerable, but no threat to the local dial-a-pizza business.' "

"I saw him pig out on Mrs. Butter's food at practically every meal," Amy said indignantly.

"And look what he says about you, Shanon," Palmer added, zeroing in on Fen's closing paragraph: " 'An unexpected bonus of my stay at Alma was the cute fourth-former who dreams of becoming a reporter someday. Armed with a video camera, she became my shadow, recording my every breath. The arrangement was a bit nerve-wracking at times, but she was such a cute kid, I did my best to be patient with her. I hope my visit provided a good learning experience for her.' "

Amy turned to the others and stuck her finger down her throat, pretending to gag. " '*Cute kid*'? Fen Hudson makes me sick."

The three girls turned to Shanon, their faces a study in disbelief and shock. She could see that they were waiting for her to say something.

"It—it's only a rough draft," Shanon stammered. "I mean, he's still working on it. Maybe he didn't take such good notes while he was here."

"I can't believe you're making excuses for him," Palmer said. "He would have had to be deaf, dumb, and blind to take notes that were *that* bad."

"I'm not making excuses for him," Shanon said, picking on a thread in her skirt. "But maybe he was purposely exaggerating a little, to make the article more dramatic. He did ask for my opinion. I'll just write to him and point out the places where he got things wrong."

"You really think he'll change it?" Max asked.

"I'm sure he will," Shanon insisted. "This is just a rough draft. I'll write him back first thing tomorrow and set him straight."

"That Fen is the biggest phony I ever met in my life!" Amy said. "He couldn't stop raving about Alma while he was here, and now he just turns around and puts us down!"

"Fen isn't a phony," Shanon replied staunchly. "He just got a little confused. That's all."

Although her friends were furious over the way Fen had trashed Alma, they suddenly realized that Shanon had more reason than any of them to feel hurt and betrayed. Knowing she still had a terrific crush on Fen, her friends could only imagine how she felt being referred to as a "cute kid."

Maxie leaned over to her roommate and gently patted her shoulder. "If he's going to listen to anyone at Alma, it would have to be you, Shanon," she said.

"I'll tell him everything you guys said," she promised. "Only, maybe we should keep this all to ourselves for now. What do you think?" she asked her suitemates.

"Shanon's right," Amy said. "Why get the whole school bent out of shape over this article when he'll probably rewrite it completely before it goes in *The Bugle*?"

Max and Palmer agreed. They knew Shanon would be mortified if anyone else saw this version of Fen's article. Most of the Alma girls had the impression that Shanon and Fen were practically going steady. It would be totally humiliating for her if everyone knew he'd referred to her as a cute but pesky kid.

"Thanks, guys," Shanon said. "I'm sure Fen will fix this article up before it goes to press. I know he would *never* want to be an inaccurate reporter."

CHAPTER FIFTEEN

"Gee, you're here early, Shanon," Kate said as she came into the *Ledger* office first thing Tuesday morning. "Working on something special?"

"Sort of," Shanon replied, not sure she wanted to confide in Kate.

Shanon had gone to the *Ledger* office at almost the crack of day to fire off her letter to Fen. As soon as it was typed, she planned to fax it to him in care of *The Bugle* office at Pewter.

Shanon quickly typed the letter, then spent a few minutes mulling over the pros and cons of letting Kate in on her secret. But before she could decide, Mr. Griffith walked into the office with Nancy, the photo editor.

"Sorry to interrupt your work, girls," he said, "but I just received something in the mail I thought you should see."

"Is that the latest issue of *The Bugle*?" Kate asked, spotting the newspaper their faculty adviser was holding. "I didn't expect to get a copy so soon."

"It arrived a little earlier than usual this week," Mr. Griffith explained. Shanon noticed he wasn't smiling and seemed uneasy as he handed the newspaper to Kate. "Fen Hudson sent it over special delivery. His article about Alma is on the front page."

"Let's see," Kate said eagerly.

"His article about Alma!" Shocked, Shanon jumped up from her seat and ran over to Kate. "It can't be," she said, her voice trailing off dismally.

It took only a glance for Shanon to see that it was the same "rough draft" Fen had sent her the day before. Not a single punctuation mark had been changed. She felt the most awful feeling in the pit of her stomach, as if someone had just punched her there.

"Why, this is the worst piece of junk I've ever read!" Kate sputtered. "The only thing he got right is the fact that Alma is located in New Hampshire. Everything else is pure baloney! He might just as well have stayed at Pewter and made it all up."

"Shanon, did you see the part he wrote about you?" Kate asked, turning to her.

"I already read it, Kate," Shanon said quietly.

"You already read it?" Kate said, sounding shocked. "When?"

"I got a copy in the mail yesterday," Shanon explained. "Fen said it was just a rough draft and he wanted my opinion. . . ."

"And you didn't tell anybody?"

"I know he got a lot of things wrong, but I thought he would revise it before it was printed. I was just going to send him a letter about it. I—" She broke off in midsentence. Her throat felt tight, and she was afraid she was going to cry.

"I guess the Pew-litzer-prize-winning editor of *The Pew-*

ter Bugle decided to go ahead without your critique," Kate said.

"I know you feel angry about the article, Kate," Mr. Griffith cut in. "I'm sure everyone at Alma will. But it's hardly Shanon's fault. You do understand that, don't you? And you, too, Shanon?"

But Shanon had already picked up her books and was dashing out of the newspaper office. She knew from the funny stares in the hallway that people could see she was crying. But she didn't care. Pretty soon everyone at Alma would know why.

Shanon practically became a hermit during the next few days. Too embarrassed to face her schoolmates, she split her time outside of classes between the shadowy corners of the library and the secluded communications lab.

Shanon knew she could hardly be blamed for Fen's article, yet it was clear that some girls considered her guilty by association. Fen Hudson was miles away, but Shanon was right there on campus, an easy target for their rage.

Toward the end of the week, Shanon and Kate were working in the *Ledger* office when a group of Alma students led by Georgette Durand appeared at the doorway and marched in.

"We've come to talk about Fen Hudson's horrible attack against Alma," Georgette said. "We want to know what *The Ledger* plans to do about it."

Kate and Shanon glanced at each other. They had already considered printing an article in *The Ledger* defending Alma, but weren't sure they should even dignify Fen's insults with a response. What would a real newspaper do?

they wondered. They had finally agreed to talk it over with Mr. Griffith at his earliest convenience.

"The editorial staff hasn't decided yet," Kate answered honestly.

"The students of Alma Stephens want *The Ledger* to fight back!" said one of the girls, handing Kate a sheaf of papers. "We've written our own response, and we want you to print it in the next issue. On the front page!"

Kate quickly looked over the article. "I can't print this," she said firmly.

"Why not?" Georgette challenged her.

"Because it's a hostile blast of hot air, even less accurate than Hudson's rubbish. Alma would be embarrassed even further by printing this," she replied, giving the papers back to Georgette. "If and when *The Ledger* replies to Fen's article about Alma, it will be done in a professional manner."

Georgette's face flushed with anger, and she started to make a sharp retort. But she bit her tongue as she realized that Kate was not about to back down. After a long moment of silence, she finally muttered, "That figures. With Shanon Davis as the star reporter, of course *The Ledger* won't print a word against Fen Hudson."

"Why don't you just write a letter to the editor, Georgette?" Kate said calmly. "But now, if you'll please excuse us, we have work to do."

"I can't believe this," Georgette sputtered as Kate herded her and the others out the door. "I'm going to tell Mr. Griffith—and Miss Pryn," she threatened.

"Tell whomever you like," Kate said. Then she shut the door firmly behind them and turned to face Shanon. "The nerve of some people! Barging in here and telling us how to run the paper."

"You were really something, Kate," Shanon told her friend.

"It was nothing," Kate said, shrugging off the compliment.

"Thanks for sticking up for me," Shanon added shyly.

"Georgette had no right to question the integrity of a *Ledger* reporter. Especially you," Kate said seriously. "Besides, I owe you an apology. I was very angry when I read Fen's article the other day, and I nearly did blame you. But I realize you had no way of stopping him. It was already on its way to the printer by the time he sent it to you. Everybody at Alma liked him and trusted him—no matter what they say now. You certainly weren't the only one."

"I guess not," Shanon said sadly.

"Don't look so down," Kate urged her. "In a week or two, everyone around here will have forgotten they ever heard the name—" Kate paused and made a sour face, as if she'd bitten into a lemon. "Well, you know who I mean."

Unfortunately, Shanon knew only too well.

CHAPTER SIXTEEN

"Shanon? Are you in here?"

From the back of the darkened communications lab, Shanon looked up to see her roommate standing in the doorway. "Back here, Max!" she called out, taking a quick look at her watch. Was it five o'clock already? The past few hours had flown by.

"It's spooky in here," Maxie said, glancing around at all the electronic equipment in the small, dim booth.

"Not really. It's fun," Shanon said. "I'm almost finished. Do you mind if I go through this last segment one more time?"

"Not at all. I'd love to see it," Maxie said, pulling up a stool. "How's it coming?"

"The masterpiece is almost finished," Shanon said dryly as both girls turned to face the monitor. Images of Fen Hudson flickered before their eyes, while the sound of Shanon's voice on audio wove them together.

"This is great," Max said after a few minutes.

"Oh, it's all right," Shanon said. "I've seen it so many times, it's practically one big blur by now." She never thought she'd admit it, even to herself, but she'd seen enough of Fen Hudson for a lifetime!

"Shanon, you're being much too modest," Max said, shaking her head. "I bet this wins first prize in the contest. Has Mr. Griffith seen it yet?"

"No. I don't want to show it to him until it's completely done." Shanon stopped the tape and hit the rewind button. "Maybe I'll give him a copy next week."

"You know, you really could have made Fen look awful in the video," Maxie reflected. "Weren't you tempted to take some revenge?"

"To tell the truth, the thought did occur to me," Shanon confessed. "But I decided against it."

It wouldn't have taken much, she knew, to make Fen look like a total dork in the video. She could easily have manipulated the images and misrepresented the facts just as he had done in his article about Alma. But just because Fen Hudson was not a good reporter didn't mean she had to lower her standards, too. That wouldn't be any kind of revenge on Fen, Shanon realized. She'd only be shortchanging herself.

Once Shanon had sorted it all out, she found it easier to work on the video. She believed she had put together a documentary that was fair and accurate. Without manipulating the facts in any way, her video showed all of Fen's statements about Alma to be false. She had done her best and had no regrets. She would be glad to put the whole project behind her.

She flicked on the lights and the two girls gathered up their books. They left the lab and hurried outside. Shanon took an appreciative gulp of fresh air. She'd spent hours cooped up in the video lab.

"Hey, before I forget, I picked something up for you at the bookstore," Maxie said as they strolled across the campus. She handed Shanon a copy of *Huck Finn*. "It was the last one left and I know you signed up for the book talk."

"Gee, thanks, Max," Shanon said. "I've been so busy with the video, I totally forgot about this. It's this week, right?"

"Thursday," Maxie said. "It should be . . . fun," she added doubtfully.

"Is Paul coming?" Shanon asked.

"I'm not sure. First he said he was, then he said he had too much studying." Max sighed. "It might be better if he didn't come. I get a little nervous when I see him," she confessed. "I like him and all that, but I guess I'm just scared."

"Scared about what?"

"I don't know." Maxie shrugged. "I never had a real boyfriend before. I guess it's scary to think you can get to know a person and really like them, but maybe it won't work out. He'll break up with you, or you'll break up with him. It almost makes me feel like I want to quit before I start. I—"

Maxie abruptly stopped talking as she suddenly realized she might be reminding Shanon of her disappointment with Fen.

"Are you thinking about me and Fen?" Shanon said, as if reading her mind.

"Not really," Maxie said. Then she paused. "Well, maybe a little bit."

"Actually," Shanon confessed, "it's Mars I miss."

"You do?" Maxie was surprised. Shanon hadn't even

mentioned Mars in weeks. Max assumed she'd forgotten all about him.

"I really do," Shanon said sadly.

When she first compared Fen and Mars, her old pen pal had seemed far less sophisticated and mature. But now Shanon saw the two boys differently. Fen was the one who didn't measure up to Mars. Mars wasn't exactly Prince Charming, that was for sure. But he would never have treated her, or Alma, the way Fen did. Maybe Mars wasn't much for compliments, but he didn't try to win people over with false flattery either. Mars was a total original, and he didn't have a phony bone in his body.

"Maybe you'll see Mars at the book-talk tea," Maxie offered.

"I doubt it," Shanon said glumly. "He hates those teas. I guess I really blew it with Mars. He probably got a big laugh out of Fen's article. I bet he thinks it served me right."

"Mars isn't like that, Shanon. He'd never laugh at your expense," Maxie said. "Why don't you send him a note? Invite him to the book talk? Maybe you guys can make up."

"I waited too long. If Mars ever sent *me* a letter like the one I sent *him,* I'd be furious. Besides," she said with a deep sigh, "I've had it with boys. I mean it, too!"

Maxie could tell from Shanon's tone that she really did mean it. At least for the moment. There was no sense in trying to talk more about Mars, Maxie realized.

Brier girls or not, Maxie was sure Mars was still crazy about Shanon—and probably still walking into walls because of the whole mess. She wondered if there was anything she could do to bring Mars and Shanon back together.

CHAPTER SEVENTEEN

"Ugh! Look at my hair!" Amy wailed. "It's freaking out!"

"What's wrong with it?" Palmer asked, barely glancing from the mirror over her dresser where she was fussing with her own hair. "It looks about usual to me."

"It's sticking up in about ten million directions at once. It looks like I just stuck my finger in a light socket. It looks terrible," Amy ranted. She pulled at her straight, spiky hair, tried on a bright green hairband, then instantly yanked it off.

"Like I said," Palmer replied with a slow smile, "it looks about usual."

"Thanks a bunch, Palmer! Just wait until you—"

But before Amy could finish her threat, Maxie walked into the room and handed Amy a tube of hair gel. "Try this. Instant relief for a frizz attack."

"My hair is too straight to be frizzy," Amy said.

"Static electricity," Max explained. "You either used too much shampoo, or your brain has been working up some high voltage about possibly seeing Nikos at the book talk."

"I *haven't* been thinking about Nikos," Amy flatly denied. She squeezed out a little gel on her fingertip and tried it out on one strand while Max watched. "Well . . . I certainly haven't been thinking about him enough to make my hair stand on end," she said. "Besides, I don't think he's coming to this thing. He doesn't like books all that much."

"Then why all the fuss about your hair?" Palmer prodded.

"Because . . . because none of your business, Palmer," Amy sputtered. The gel was working out fine, and she dabbed some more on the rest of her hair. Then she turned a critical eye to her outfit. She was wearing a yellow cotton turtleneck covered with black polka dots, a black cotton miniskirt, and matching tights that had black and yellow horizontal stripes on one leg and black with yellow polka dots on the other.

"I think your outfit is really cool," Maxie said.

"Thanks, I love your tie," Amy returned the compliment. Max was wearing an oversized gray tweed blazer, a pale lilac shirt with a big wide, wild print tie, a denim miniskirt, black tights, and purple suede loafers. "Paul is going to forget all about Huck Finn once he gets a look at you," she whispered.

"Paul isn't coming," Maxie said, looking down. "He wrote and said he changed his mind."

"That's too bad," Amy said sympathetically. "It looks like we're all in the same boat. What a drag! We get to have a book-talk tea with Ardsley boys and all we're going to do is drink tea . . . and talk about books!"

"There are other boys who go to Ardsley besides Nikos, Paul, and Mars," Palmer pointed out.

"I guess so," Amy said, putting a shiny round black

earring on her left ear and a square yellow one on her right. She didn't sound very convinced. "Like I said before, this is going to be a total snore."

"You guys ready yet?" Shanon asked, popping her head into the room. "I just saw the bus from Ardsley pull up."

Shanon was wearing her slim white denim jeans and a peach-colored cotton sweater that complemented her rosy complexion and hazel eyes.

While her suitemates chatted about their hair and outfits in the bedroom, Shanon had been glued to the big sitting-room window, watching for the Ardsley bus. But then it pulled up so close to the building that she couldn't really see who had gotten off, only that there were a lot of Ardies invading Fox Hall. She couldn't help wishing that Mars were one of them.

Carrying pads, pens, and their copies of *Huck Finn,* the four Foxes hurried downstairs. Palmer led the way into the lounge, quickly scanned the room for the cutest available boy, and took off in his direction.

The other girls stopped near the doorway, each thinking about the particular face she would not find in the crowd. "Who wants some tea and cookies?" Amy asked. "I hope Mrs. Butter made her special shortbread. How about it, Shanon? Maxie . . . ?"

But Maxie wasn't listening. "Look! Over near the window," she yelped, gripping Amy's arm. "Do you see what I *think* I see?"

"Oh, my gosh!" Amy said, making a great effort to keep her voice down.

Shanon's eyes darted across the room and her stomach did a double back flip.

CHAPTER EIGHTEEN

———◆———

Mars was standing near the window with Nikos and Paul. All three boys looked perfectly at ease, talking and eating cookies, then brushing the crumbs off their blue Ardsley blazers and red ties.

"I thought they weren't coming," Shanon whispered.

"Good thing we dressed up anyway," Maxie whispered back.

Nikos was the first to notice Amy, Max, and Shanon standing near the doorway. He gave them a big smile before turning back to his friends. The other two boys instantly looked across the room. Then Paul and Nikos began to walk over, but Mars hung back. He waved to Shanon, took another bite of his cookie, and looked down at his shoes.

For one wonderful but terrifying moment, Shanon thought Mars was going to walk over, too. But when he didn't, she felt her face fall. He obviously hadn't come to the book talk to see her. Maybe he had a date with some other Alma girl, Shanon speculated sadly.

Paul and Maxie quickly drifted off in one direction. Amy

and Nikos stood and talked with Shanon for a while, and then Amy pulled him off in another direction. She had something important to say to Nikos and she figured she might as well get it over with right away. But then she thought, maybe it would be better to wait. Once Nikos found out how she really felt about his painting, he might never want to see her again. Still, she'd have to tell him something.

Before she could lose her nerve, she cleared her throat loudly and began: "I'm glad you came, Nikos. I have to talk to you about that painting you did of me and—"

"Amy," Nikos interrupted her, "before you say anything else, there's something I have to tell you. It's about that painting."

Amy felt her cheeks redden—this wasn't going to be easy—but Nikos wasn't looking at her. He was staring down at the floor unhappily.

"I know how much you like the portrait, and I know I promised it was going to be reproduced in the literary magazine, but I'm afraid I spoke too soon. The art editor of the *Aurora* has no taste at all! He decided to use some boring sketch of an oak tree instead. I hope you aren't too disappointed," he said, finally looking her full in the face.

"An oak tree, instead of me? I'm crushed," Amy said with a dazzling smile of relief. "But don't feel bad," she said generously. "I know it isn't your fault."

Across the room, Shanon was standing all alone when a boy she'd never seen before came striding purposefully toward her.

"Hey, are you Shanon Davis?" he asked without even saying hello.

"Yes." Shanon nodded.

"You're the girl who made a video of that Pew guy who totally trashed Alma in *The Bugle?*"

"Everything he wrote about Alma in that article was wrong!" Shanon said firmly.

"Sure," he said sarcastically. "That's what all you girls are saying."

"None of it was true," Shanon insisted. "Alma is a wonderful school," she said sincerely. But when he just repeated "Sure" in the same disbelieving tone, she excused herself and hurried to the other side of the room. Plopping herself down on a sofa near the fireplace, she buried her nose in her copy of *Huck Finn.* If anyone else had something to say about Fen Hudson, she didn't want to hear it.

But Shanon couldn't help overhearing snatches of the conversations going on all around her between Ardsley boys and Alma Stephens girls, and she couldn't help noticing that nobody in the room was talking about good old Huckleberry Finn. The hot topic of conversation at this book talk was not Finn—it was Fen and his infamous article about Alma!

The Ardie boys were having a field day putting down Alma, while the girls were doing their best to convince them that Fen's article was totally unfair and untrue.

Shanon lifted her book higher, completely covering her face. This had to be the worst day of her life! Why had she ever signed up for this book talk? Of course, she knew the answer to that question. She'd signed up on the slim chance that Mars would somehow show up. And there he was, across the room, talking to Maxie and Paul. But he might as well have been on the South Pole for all the good it was doing her.

"Shanon, are you all right?" It was Maxie, sitting down next to her on the couch.

"You look a little pale. How about a cookie?" Amy asked, sitting down on the other side.

"I'm okay, I guess," Shanon said unconvincingly.

"I wish everyone would stop talking about stupid Fen Hudson and his stupid article!" Amy whispered.

"That makes two of us." Shanon sighed. She took a huge bite of the cookie Amy handed her, then turned to say something to Max. But her roommate had disappeared. Probably looking for Paul again, Shanon thought.

"How are things going with Nikos?" she asked Amy.

"Great!" Amy said with a grin. "My portrait isn't going to be in the magazine after all," she whispered. "Oops, here he comes. I'll tell you all about it later."

"Hey, take a look over there," Nikos said, walking up to Amy and Shanon. He pointed to the other side of the room. "Why is everyone watching TV? I thought we were here to talk about books."

At the other end of the room, a large group had gathered around the big new television monitor. Along with Amy and Nikos, Shanon strolled over to see what they were watching with such great interest.

But before she could see anything, Shanon recognized the sound of her own voice! With a heart-stopping jolt she realized it was her video.

"Oh, no!" Shanon cried, grabbing Amy's arm. "How did *that* get on the TV?"

"I don't know, but let's get closer. I can hardly see it from here," Amy said, practically dragging Shanon toward the front of the group.

In stunned silence, Shanon watched her vision of Fen flash across the screen: Fen brushing his teeth and fussing over his hair in the bathroom as a girl barged in—a scene that was greeted by giggles and wisecracks from the audience. Fen sitting side by side with Alma students and discussing the causes of World War I in a history class was proof positive that the girls were extremely sharp, competitive, and creative. Hardly the way he had described them in his article.

Shanon pushed her way through the crowd to turn the video off. Who could have put it on like this without her permission? Her life at Alma was miserable enough these days. But if her classmates hated her video, it could get even worse!

She was just reaching for the stop button when Mr. Griffith stepped in front of her. "Don't turn that off, Shanon," he said gently. "Let's see what you've done."

"I'd rather show it to you privately," Shanon replied, blinking back the tears that were welling up in her eyes.

"Why? It looks good," Mr. Griffith said. He placed a hand on her shoulder before adding, "Besides, I have a feeling the audience would raise quite a ruckus if you turned it off now. Take a look. They're really enjoying it."

Shanon had been so absorbed in the images on the screen, she hadn't been at all aware of the audience's reaction. Now she turned to look at the students who were watching her work. Mr. Griffith wasn't just trying to make her feel good. It was true. Everybody did look very interested.

One of her interview segments with Fen had come on. Now Shanon was glad that she hadn't given in to the temptation to manipulate the facts just for a moment of revenge. Watching the video, she felt proud of her work. It was an honest portrait of Fen Hudson's visit and of Alma Stephens's brand of education. Alma looked good, no doubt about it. Surely everyone in the room could see how badly Fen's article had misrepresented the students, faculty, and academic spirit of her school. . . .

"Great job!" Mr. Griffith said when the video was over. "I think you have a solid entry here, Shanon."

"Thanks," Shanon said shyly.

Everyone was applauding. She could hardly believe it. She hung back at the edge of the crowd, overhearing good reviews of her work and even some apologetic remarks from the Ardsley boys who, moments ago, had been criticizing Alma.

Shanon was trying so hard to hear all their comments that she didn't even realize the Ardsley boy she knew best of all was heading her way.

CHAPTER NINETEEN

"Don't be mad Shanon. It was all my idea, honest," a familiar voice blurted out.

"What?" Shocked, Shanon turned to see Mars standing beside her.

"I hope you're not too upset about us showing your video like that," Mars began in a rush. "But when Max told me and Paul that she'd seen part of your video and it proved Fen Hudson's article was all wrong, I persuaded her to get it out of your desk and then I put it on." When Shanon didn't say anything, Mars went on: "*Are* you angry?"

"No. . . ." Shanon shook her head. She had a feeling she *should* be angry, but she really wasn't. "At least these Ardies know the real truth about Alma now. They can see for themselves it's as good a school as Pewter."

"Maybe even better," Mars added with a bright smile. He looked awfully relieved that Shanon wasn't mad. He looked awfully cute today, too, Shanon reflected. "Want to go for a walk?" he asked hopefully.

"Sure," Shanon said. She couldn't believe the sudden

turn the day was taking. A few moments ago she had been totally depressed. Now she felt like jumping for joy.

Shanon and Mars slipped out of Fox Hall and walked wordlessly toward the river. Shanon felt her pulse racing and hoped Mars couldn't tell how nervous she felt. It was wonderful to see him again. She had missed him so much. She was sorry now for making such a big deal about Fen in her letters and hurting his feelings. She had so much to say, but she didn't know where to begin. The words seemed stuck in her throat.

"I was really smoking mad when I read that dumb article in *The Bugle*," Mars finally broke the silence. "The nerve of that guy. The way he put you down, it just made me so angry!"

"It did?" Shanon asked. She had never seen Mars so steamed up about anything. She'd had no idea he cared so much about her. For once, he wasn't making a joke about it.

"Of course it did," he insisted. "Calling you a 'cute kid' and all that garbage! You're no 'cute kid,'" he said, taking her hand. "You're smart, sweet, pretty. . . . Don't you realize I think you're the most terrific person I know?"

"You do?" Shanon stared up at Mars in disbelief. Could this be a dream or was her old pen pal really saying all those things she had longed to hear?

"Of course I do. I really missed you," he said softly.

"I missed you, too. A lot," Shanon confessed.

"You seemed so excited about that Hudson creep," Mars said, looking out at the river for a second. "I didn't know what to think."

"I guess I was kind of bowled over by him at first," Shanon said honestly. "But he didn't turn out to be anything like I thought. If I never see him again in my entire life, it will be too soon." Shanon hesitated a moment. Then she took a deep breath and asked, "How about those girls from Brier? The *dedicated* and *admirable* ones, I mean?"

"Oh, them." Mars shook his head. "I did start volunteering, but I made up all that other stuff just to make you jealous."

"Well . . . it worked," Shanon said simply. It was easy to be honest with Mars now that she knew how much he cared for her. It felt great to be so open and share feelings so honestly. She had been wrong about Mars. He was a lot more mature than she'd realized.

"I'm sorry I resorted to such childish tactics. I think I owe you an apology for something else, too," Mars added. Holding her hand in both of his, he twined their fingers together. "For the clothespin gag, I mean."

"Oh, that!" Shanon laughed now, thinking about it. "It was actually pretty funny. I can't imagine why I got so bent out of shape over it."

"Well, I have something to make up for it," Mars said. With a sly look he reached into his pocket and handed Shanon a manila envelope. "Here, this is a special present for you. Go ahead, open it," he coaxed her.

Shanon reached inside the envelope to find a giant red plastic clip, the kind used at the top of clipboards to hold papers in place. A big white tag attached to it read: IN THE EVENT OF AN EMERGENCY, APPLY TO MARS MARTINEZ'S MOUTH, AS NEEDED.

Shanon burst out laughing, and so did Mars.

"Why, Mars, what a *thoughtful* gift," she teased him. "I'll cherish it forever."

"I'm glad you like it," Mars said with his wonderful

zany grin. "The perfect gift for the girl who's got everything," he added, looking suddenly serious. It was a look that made Shanon forget what she was about to say next.

Staring into her eyes, he rested his hands lightly at her waist. Then he leaned over and kissed her. Shanon's arm slipped around his back and she hugged him close. This had to be the most wonderful moment of her life. Now that she knew Mars really cared for her, Shanon thought, she definitely did have everything!

PEN PALS

PEN PALS #6: AMY'S SONG

Amy, Palmer, Shanon, and Lisa go on a class trip to London.

PEN PALS #7: HANDLE WITH CARE

Shanon runs for student council president—against Lisa.

PEN PALS #8: SEALED WITH A KISS

Amy stars in a rock musical with Lisa's pen pal Rob.

PEN PALS #9: STOLEN PEN PALS

Four girls from a rival school try to steal the Foxes' pen pals.

PEN PALS #10: PALMER AT YOUR SERVICE

When her parents cut her allowance, Palmer has to take a waitress job.

PEN PALS #11: ROOMMATE TROUBLE

Lisa thinks Shanon's new friend Lorraine is taking advantage of her.

PEN PALS #12: LISA'S SECRET

Lisa is afraid her parents are getting a divorce.

PEN PALS #13: LISA, WE MISS YOU

Amy, Shanon, and Palmer get a new suitemate named Maxine Schloss.

PEN PALS #14: THE MYSTERY ABOUT MAXIE

Maxie has a mysterious pen pal.

PEN PALS SUPER SPECIAL #1: DREAM HOLIDAY

Palmer, Amy, and Shanon go to Maxie's New York townhouse for the Christmas party of their dreams!

PEN PALS #15: THE HEARTBREAK GUY

Amy auditions for a local rock band—and falls for the lead singer!

PEN PALS #16: BOY CRAZY

Palmer has her eye on Maxie's new, rich pen pal. Maxie won't mind, or will she?

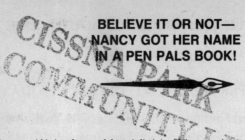

BELIEVE IT OR NOT—
NANCY GOT HER NAME
IN A PEN PALS BOOK!

Nancy Weis from Marshfield, Wisconsin, wrote PEN PALS headquarters and told us about herself and her pen pal Jessica Heller. Nancy spends most of her time writing to Jessica, and reading in her bedroom. Her older sister believes that one day Nancy will become an author! Good luck!

Congratulations, Nancy! Check out page 94 in book #17, *The Boy Project,* and you'll find that a character has been named after you. The character named Nancy is photo editor of *The Ledger.* Don't thank us, Nancy. Thank Sharon Dennis Wyeth for making your name famous!

Every month, Sharon Dennis Wyeth, the author of the PEN PALS series, names a character in one of her books after a PEN PALS reader. If you'd like to have a character named after you, write in and let us know what's going on with you and your pen pal. What do you guys actually *say* in your letters? Are you making any exciting plans to call or visit your pen pals?

Don't write back soon, write now! Send your letters to:

PEN PALS HEADQUARTERS
c/o PARACHUTE PRESS
156 FIFTH AVE. ROOM 325
NEW YORK, NY 10010

People *really do* get Pen Pals! The pen pals you'll read about below are having a ball writing to one another. So get into the act—don't let these kids have all the fun!

Shannon Balentine of Caribou, Maine, is writing to Nicole Gagnon of Prince George, British Columbia, Canada.